EMMA'S WAR

Book Two

TUG-BOAT ANNIE!

DEDICATION

Dedicated to my grandchildren
— K. H. I. and J.
and to 'Bill,' 'Fran' and 'Jonty'
with many thanks for their shared memories

BY THE SAME AUTHOR

Book Two

Tug-Boat Annie!

VIOLET BRAND

EGON

EGON PUBLISHERS LTD

Published in 1991
Second impression 1992
Third impression 1994
by Egon Publishers Ltd,
Royston Road, Baldock, Herts SG7 6NW

ISBN 0 905858 59 X

Illustrations by Tony Richards

Designed and printed in Great Britain by
Streetsprinters,
Royston Road, Baldock,
Herts SG7 6NW

Contents

INTRODUCTION

VIOLET BRAND was ten years old when the war broke out. She lived in Canterbury, Kent and vividly remembers the Battle of Britain fought overhead during the summer of 1940, then the sudden evacuation of children in September, due to an invasion scare.

She and her family returned to Canterbury, after four months in Reading and, like many others, were there during the Blitz on June 1st, 1942. Her own school was destroyed that night and the school of her younger brother and sister was damaged by incendiary bombs.

The air raid siren, Tug-Boat Annie (the noise which issued forth to tell them that enemy planes were overhead) and air raid shelters, were part of everyday life, as were the tragedies that struck the families of friends. Barrage balloons and the havoc they could cause will never be forgotten.

The final years of the war brought other experiences and inevitably, nothing could separate those which were part of a teenager's life within the family and those which were the direct result of the Second World War.

She says that between 1939 and 1945 she was often very scared, but never bored. It was impossible to know what the next day would bring.

She was one of a family of four children and it is on their experiences that 'Emma's War' is based. Canterbury and Kenabury, home of 'Emma's' family, have much in common. The Dane John park with its burial mound and the lofty cathedral which remained almost untouched, despite the destruction of many surrounding buildings, are as much part of Canterbury today, as they were of the 'Kenabury' where 'Emma' lived during the war.

The social conditions which were common to all working-class families, would have been the same irrespective of the war — and the strong community spirit always exisited.

Violet Brand has manipulated some dates, places, events and people to ensure that the effects of the war on one family growing up between 1939–45, will be meaningful to children growing up in the 1990s — including her own grandchildren.

Chapter One

BLASTS AND BANGS

THE noise, like an angry bull, woke Emma up with a start. She shook Fran.

'Get up. It's gone,' she said.

'What's gone?' mumbled Fran.

'Tug-Boat Annie,' replied Emma urgently.

'Come on you girls. Quick. Down the shelter,' called Dad.

'We're not dressed,' they wailed.

'Forget clothes,' he said. 'Get down those stairs!'

Shivering with fright, not cold, the two girls grabbed dressing gowns, forgot slippers and rushed downstairs, out into the garden. They climbed down the rickety steps into the dark, musty air-raid shelter and sat shivering on their bunks.

'You boys. Get up and get out.' Dad was shouting at Bill and Jonty.

The planes roared overhead and through the open shelter door the girls could see the search lights wheeling round in the sky, crossing and uncrossing.

'Now, be careful. Don't be scared,' said Mum's gentle voice talking to Fanny Farmer, the old lady who lived next door.

Dad had to get the family up. Mum had to go next door and deal with the elderly, grumpy neighbour. They were not sure who had the most difficult job!

Slowly, Fanny Farmer climbed in, whilst the boys hopped around outside, not sure that they actually *wanted* to get into the dark hole. It was much more exciting outside.

Finally, Fanny was in, shaking on the bunk next to Emma. The boys did not immediately climb down the steps after her and Mum.

The planes roared on — bang, crash, boom, crash. The boys and Dad tumbled in, shutting the door fast behind them. It was pitch dark.

'Where's the torch?' asked Dad.

Mum switched it on and Dad lit a single candle. The torch went off and the flickering flame was the only light.

Bang — cr–ash!

The ground shook and nasty smells drifted under the shelter door.

'Wonder what's happening out there,' mumbled Bill.

Emma could feel her knees bobbing up and down with fright, whilst her teeth chattered. She *could* not speak.

Fanny Farmer quavered, 'Offer up a prayer.' Mum cuddled Jonty and held Fran's hand.

'Time for a sing-song,' announced Dad. 'Come on.'

> 'This old man,
> He played one . . .'

One after the other, they joined in with trembling voices. By the time they had reached ten, the voices were much stronger and almost blotted out the blasts and bangs outside.

Hardly stopping to take a breath, Dad took out his mouth organ, which was usually hiding in one of his pockets. He started playing —

> 'There were ten in the bed,
> And the little one said . . .'

An *enormous* bang accompanied him, but he did not stop even though the notes trembled a bit as he played — 'Roll over.'

Smells and smoke crept under the door. He stopped, 'I think I'd better just look out,' he said.

Putting his tin hat on his head, he gently tried to open the door. It would hardly move, as if something heavy was against it.

He pushed a bit harder and dust and smoke swept in, making them cough and splutter.

'Stay there,' he commanded in a strong voice — and crept out.

They heard his voice outside, followed by the loud voice of Mr King, the air-raid warden.

'Your house has copped it,' said Mr King. 'Most of the windows have gone — and half the roof is off.'

The voices became fainter, as Dad and Mr King obviously went off to look at the damage. Miraculously, the tug-boat sounded its awful bullish sound, followed soon after by the 'All Clear' of the siren. As the sounds wailed away, the boys jumped up to go out.

'Stay where you are,' said Mum quietly, 'until Dad comes to tell us what to do.'

They waited — and waited.

Emma woke with a start, as Dad climbed into the shelter. She had dropped off to sleep. In fact everyone, except Mum, was stretching and rubbing eyes. Then they remembered Mr King's words. *Their* house had 'copped it'.

Where would they go?

What would they do?

No house to live in.

Dad sat at the bottom of the rickety steps and began to talk.

'I'm afraid our house is a bit of a mess. There are hardly any windows and most of the roof has gone. The inside's covered with bricks, soot and glass.'

Emma drew a deep noisy breath. Fran began to cry, 'Where shall we go? What shall we do?'

'Can you mend it, Dad?' asked Bill. 'I'll help.' He was almost fourteen and feeling pretty grown-up.

'Thanks Bill,' said Dad, 'I'm sure I'll need some help. But now, you're all going to the old school for hot drinks. They've got blankets up there, so you can curl up on the floor and get some more sleep.'

'Can't I go into the house first?' asked Mum.

'I'd rather you didn't,' said Dad. 'Perhaps later.'

'What about me and my house?' quavered Fanny Farmer.

'Your house is a bit like ours, so you should go to the old school as well,' said Dad. 'They *are* expecting you.'

'I'm not going up there,' declared Fanny. 'No-one's getting me out of my home — and that's that.'

'It's only whilst they mend the roof and clean it up,' said Mum in her most persuasive voice.

'They'll have to drag me out,' said Fanny. 'Take me in — I'll sit in my chair and they can clean up round me.' There was a stunned silence.

'It's bad enough,' she went on, 'crawling into this hole with you lot. I'm certainly not going to sleep in any old school with a crowd of strangers.'

'You *can't* go back in,' said Dad firmly.

'*No-one* is going to stop me — not even you!' declared Fanny, equally firmly.

'Right, kids. Emergency clothes on.' said Dad.

They scrambled under the bunks for the old trousers, jerseys, socks and shoes that had been put there for emergencies like this. Fortunately, in the flickering light of the candle, they could not see how awful they looked —and at this moment, they did not really care.

Dad helped Bill and Jonty to crawl out. Emma and Fran heard their startled voices and wondered what the boys had seen.

'Come on girls,' said Dad. 'Come carefully. There's a lot of rubbish around out here.'

Emma climbed up the rickety steps. Then she knew! The sky was bright red — not black. It was still night, but the sky was alight.

She could see piles of smoking bricks and smashed glass. She looked all round and could not see a single house with a roof.

It was the most frightening sight she had ever seen — as if there had been an earthquake on Guy Fawkes Night. But, this was *their street* — *their house*.

What was the bright light? Why was the sky red? She looked up at Dad, who saw her worried face and said, 'I'm afraid, my pet, that the High Street is on fire.'

'*All* of it?' stammered Bill.

'Well, half of it at least,' said Dad.

'Have the shops gone?' asked Bill, obviously shocked.

'Yes, lots of the shops,' answered Dad.

'But my school's behind the shops,' burst out Emma.

'Yes,' said Dad gently. 'I think your school has gone too.'

Emma began to cry. 'I left *everything* there yesterday — my new satchel, pens, books, games kit — everything. I didn't have any homework, so didn't bother to bring my things home. Do you think they've *all* gone, Dad?'

'Probably, love. We'll find out later,' said Dad.

'But what about my school?' asked Bill. 'That's next door.'

'I think half of it's left,' said Dad. 'We'll see in the morning.'

'Don't like school much anyway,' said Bill. 'If there's no school, p'raps I'll be able to leave and do a *proper* job.'

'Come on, let Mum out,' said Dad. 'Go with her to the old school and we'll see about everything else in the morning.'

Mum climbed out and Emma watched her face, as she saw the sky and the piles of rubble — then, their own house. Emma knew that Mum wanted to cry, just as *she* had cried. But, as she watched, she saw Mum's face return to its usual gentle look. She gave them all a kiss, including Dad.

'I may not have the house, but I've got all of you,' she said. 'Come on, let's go.'

She took hold of Jonty's hand and they began to climb over the piles of rubble.

'I wish you luck,' she whispered to Dad. 'You'll need it! Fanny's in one of her most difficult moods. I'm glad it's my turn for the children.' They smiled at each other and Dad said; 'Go on. Take care. Things are still falling from roofs and fires are still burning, even up here. See you later.'

They clambered slowly out of the garden, up the alley and into the street, or at least, it had been a street yesterday. Now, you could not see pavements and the road — just heaps of rubble.

Emma, Fran and the boys stopped feeling tired. Here they were, in the middle of the night, stumbling slowly along the street. It was frightening — but exciting. They saw other people stumbling along too.

'Hi, Dick,' called Bill, as his friend Dick Petts crept out from nowhere. 'Where are you going?'

'Up to the old school,' mumbled Dick. 'Don't want to go. Rather stay with Dad, but he insists.'

'Yeah, me too,' moaned Bill. 'Dad wouldn't let me stay either.' Emma did not remember hearing him pleading to stay.

'Still,' she thought, 'that's boys. Showing off. Pretending they're brave. But really, they're no braver than me.'

Chapter Two

PEOPLE AS WELL AS HOUSES

At last they reached the old school. It had never taken so long to get there. Ten minutes was the usual time, but tonight, through the rubble, surrounded by horrid smells and a frighteningly bright sky, it had felt like hours.

Lots of people were helping each other along and the adults were whispering — not talking in normal voices. Even Bill and Dick had stopped shouting. Fran and Jonty were crying.

They were probably very tired, as well as scared.

The path up to the old school felt surprisingly normal — no different to the way it had always felt. The school still perched on top of the hill and did not seem to be damaged at all. The heavy wooden doors were wide open but no friendly lights shone out. No lights shone out of *any* buildings these days.

If they did, Mr King, or another air-raid warden, would rap the door and shout, 'Put that light out!'

'That's why it feels so strange tonight,' thought Emma. 'The sky is alight, but not with friendly lights.'

She shivered as she thought of the bombed buildings and the people who might have been trapped in those buildings by fire.

'I hope, I hope,' she thought desperately, 'that no-one I know is in the fire. That would be terrible — terrible.'

She felt her legs trembling again, as they walked through the school cloakroom. The pegs were empty, and yet it sounded as though there were a lot of people in the old school. The voices were not noisy, just a quiet mumble. They had not left their coats on pegs, because they did not have any to leave.

'Just like us,' thought Emma.

Mum opened the big door into the school. It looked the same — but different. The high pitched ceiling, the big, black stove with its metal guard in the middle of the room, these were the same. But the old desks had all been pushed back into one corner of Miss Hogben's room, half hidden by the brown curtains that divided one classroom from another. Floor space was filled with people sleeping, or trying to sleep, on blankets.

Next to the big, black stove was a table with some ladies in ARP* uniform standing with huge tea pots. Piles of cups and saucers, jugs of milk and bowls of sugar were ready.

'A cup of tea first, I think,' said Mum. 'I could do with some tea to wash the dust out of my throat.'

'Does it *have* to be tea?' wailed Fran. 'I don't like tea.'

'Don't suppose there's anything else, except water,' said Mum.

'Sorry, Mrs Bart, but they can't drink water unless it's been boiled,' said one of the ARP ladies.

She obviously knew Mum.

'Why not?' asked Mum. 'What's happened to the water?'

* ARP — Air Raid Precautions.

'Well,' went on the ARP lady, 'pipes have been damaged. Some have burst and they think the water might be polluted with all the rubble around. We don't want a lot of upset tummies, beside our other troubles.'

'No. You're right,' said Mum.

'I'll tell you what,' said the lady, 'would they like hot Bovril instead of tea? I've got a big jar here.'

'Yes please. Yes please,' they all said.

'Much better than boring old tea,' said Bill.

When Mum had her tea and the four of them had their Bovril, an ARP lady came over with paper and pencil to take some details. Emma heard their voices droning on as she finished her drink and drifted off to sleep just where she was sitting.

She woke suddenly and heard Mum quietly crying beside her. She reached out her hand and said, 'What's up Mum? Is it the house?'

'No pet, not the house. People are more important than houses,' Mum replied through her tears.

'But we're all O.K. Is it someone else?' asked Emma gently.

'I wasn't going to tell you just yet — but you'll hear soon enough. It's the Turners,' said Mum, in a low, disturbed voice.

'The Turners?' Emma sounded startled. 'What, *all* of them?'

'Well, all except Jimmy,' replied Mum.

'Poor Jimmy — to lose *everyone*,' Emma could feel the sobs rising in her throat. 'How — how did he escape?'

'Jimmy's never been exactly an obedient boy,' smiled Mum. 'Instead of going to the Morrison shelter indoors, like the others, he ran off to the shelter in the Dane John*.

* Dane John is a park in Kenabury.

'A bomb hit their house — they were all killed — except Jimmy in the Dane John.'

'Poor Jimmy,' said Emma again. 'No Mum and Dad.'

Then — 'What about Betty?' she asked urgently.

'Sorry pet. Betty *was* in the house,' said Mum in a very gentle voice.

'Oh Mum,' sobbed Emma and cuddled up *very* close. 'She was my best friend — my *very* best friend.'

'I know,' said Mum. 'Remember — her Mum was *my* best friend. We've both lost someone very special.'

'And Jimmy's lost them all — and his home. Where's he going to live?' asked Emma.

'That's what I've been wondering,' said Mum. 'No-one is sure. I've suggested they bring him here to be with us. Hope you all won't mind.'

'Oh no. If it had happened to us, I know the Turners would have wanted to help,' said Emma.

'What about Bill?' asked Mum. Bill was snoring away on the floor, wrapped in a blanket.

'Yeah,' said Emma thoughtfully. 'He and Jimmy have been rivals more than friends. P'raps he'll make a big effort — 'cos I don't think Jimmy will be able to.'

'No,' said Mum. 'I think Jimmy will be naughtier than ever — or so quiet that we don't recognise him. Let's wait and see.'

She stood up. 'Come on. Let's have another drink' —and she and Emma went across to the lady with the teapots.

As they wrapped their hands around the warm cups, they jumped violently. Tug-Boat Annie sounded out its fierce unwelcome noise.

Hot Bovril and tea spilled over — it hurt. Sleepers woke with a start and jumped up grabbing blankets.

'Where do we go?' they shouted. 'Where are the shelters?'

The wail of the siren joined with Tug-Boat Annie and the roar of planes began almost immediately. Guns boomed and Emma felt herself panic.

'Not again. Not again,' she pleaded. She wanted to curl up on the floor with a blanket wrapped tightly round her ears so that she could not hear *anything*. If only she could blot it all out.

'Quick — across the road and into the Dane John shelter,' ordered the ARP warden.

'Hurry up there,' he shouted to the sleepy people. 'We may not have much time.'

Bang! Cr–ash! 'That's what it felt like before,' thought Emma, shaking with fright.

'Grab Fran,' said Mum. 'Bill bring some blankets.' She

took hold of Jonty and they joined the others in the scramble for the door.

Out in the school yard, the sky was still alight. Standing out in the red glare was the perfect shape of the cathedral.

'Perhaps that's what they've come back for,' said Emma to Bill.

'Better that than people being killed,' he replied.

'Do you know about the Turners?' Emma asked in a whisper. He had been asleep when she and Mum had been talking.

'No,' he said, looking startled. 'What about the Turners?'

He did not speak softly and Mum turned round and said, 'Not now Emma. I'll tell him later.'

'What about the Turners?' piped up Fran.

'Later,' said Mum firmly.

They reached the Dane John shelter just as a terrifying explosion shook the ground.

'Run!' said Mum, and they all ran as fast as they could to the safety of the shelter.

It was gloomy inside and smelt damp and dirty — not surprising, when it was mounds of soil supported by props and sand bags.

In the faint lights, they could vaguely see the rough benches filled with people. Further off, they could hear the sound of singing.

'Keep walking,' said Mum, 'towards the singing.'

Chapter Three

OLD MIKE

AFTER they had squeezed their way between hundreds of knees, they reached the far end of the shelter where a crowd of people of all ages were sitting and standing round Old Mike.

Old Mike used to be the banana man before the war, pushing his barrow, piled high with bananas, from house to house. Everyone liked Old Mike. He was always smiling and cheerful. He did not push his barrow around now, for since the war had started, there *were* no bananas.

Emma remembered the time when there was a knock on the door on her birthday. She had just come out of hospital and had a big bandage round her head. She felt a bit miserable, even though it *was* her birthday.

Old Mike said, 'Hold out your pinny*,' — and he piled it high with bananas. 'That's towards your party.'

Emma remembered how happy she felt and that those were the last bananas she had seen — the war had just started.

'Trust Old Mike to be in the shelter cheering everyone up in this awful air-raid,' she thought.

* Pinafore, or apron.

Like Dad, he kept a mouth-organ in his pocket and, as they joined the group, she heard him saying, 'Come on. Whatever it's like out there — SING. You'll feel much better.'

> 'Pack up your troubles
> In your old kit-bag
> And smile, smile, smile,' he played.

They smiled as they sang in very loud voices to shut out the bangs and crashes, booms and whines that went on unceasingly outside.

There was one person who was not singing. Some-one was curled up next to Old Mike. The face was covered with a blanket, so that no-one could see who it was. It did not look like an adult.

'Someone about the same size as Bill,' thought Emma. She froze with horror at the thought — and stopped singing.

'It's Jimmy. I *know* it's Jimmy. He's hiding from everyone — but he wanted to be near someone safe — Old Mike. I don't blame him,' thought Emma. 'I'd feel safe with Old Mike. Even though he's always cheery, I know he'd understand.'

She pulled at Mum's jersey. Mum stopped singing and bent her head down to listen.

'Mum,' she whispered, 'I think that's Jimmy hiding in the blanket.'

Mum looked across at the bundle. 'I'm sure you're right,' she said. 'He must feel terrible.'

'It's not like Jimmy to be hiding — he's always in the middle of everything.' Emma wanted to cry again and she could see tears running down Mum's face.

Bill looked round. 'What's up, you two?' he asked, puzzled by the tears.

Mum said to Emma, 'Hold on to Fran and Jonty. Come with me, Bill. I want to talk to you.'

Emma tried to sing again, holding tightly on to the other two, whilst Mum and Bill crept away out of earshot.

The bangs and crashes seemed to have stopped and above the sound of singing, Emma could hear Tug-boat Annie bellowing out the 'All Clear,' followed almost immediately by the more cheerful sound of the siren's single note.

Cheering burst out.

'All O-VER!' shouted Old Mike.

The bundle in the blanket shot up.

'It's not "ALL OVER" — it's just started!' burst out Jimmy Turner. His white face looked hurt and angry. Before anyone could say, or do, anything, he huddled down again and pulled the blanket right over his head.

Emma could see the blanket heaving and shaking. She knew Jimmy must be crying and she began to cry too. Old

24

Mike's hand rested gently on the huddled shape. He was murmuring something. Emma could not hear what, but she was sure that Jimmy would feel comforted by the soft sounds and protective hand.

People stood around awkwardly at first, not knowing what to do, or say. They knew they wanted to help Jimmy but just did not know how.

Old Mike waved to them with his free hand, silently saying, 'Goodbye. Go home. I'll look after Jimmy.'

At that moment Mum and Bill reappeared. Bill looked as if he had been crying and Mum's arm was round his shoulders.

As she came up, Old Mike beckoned to her.

'Wait here, all of you. I'll go and have a word with Mike,' she said.

Bill, Emma, Fran and Jonty watched as they talked together very quietly. Mum nodded, shook her head and nodded again. She and Old Mike squeezed hands and then she returned.

'We'll go back to the old school now,' she said.

'What's happening to Jimmy?' asked Bill.

'I'll tell you later,' said Mum as they made their way back between the empty wooden benches and emerged from the dim shelter into the early morning sunshine.

Looking towards the High Street, the sky was still bright red.

'It's O.K.,' breathed Emma.

'What's O.K.?' asked Mum as they climbed the sloping path to the school.

'The cathedral. It's still there. They didn't get it, the first, or second time,' she replied.

'No, they didn't get the cathedral,' said Mum in a sad voice.

25

'They got the Turners though,' said Bill, viciously kicking a stone.

They walked through the cloakroom and then opened the big heavy door. Dad was standing by the tea table, his hands wrapped round a steaming mug. Jonty rushed over to him, nearly scalding himself as the mug wobbled in Dad's hands.

Putting the mug down. Dad picked him up and hugged him. Jonty flung his arms round Dad's neck.

'I'm *so* glad to see you,' he said. 'Everything's all right again, now that we're all here.'

They crowded round to hear what Dad had to say. Mum slipped her hand under his arm, as if she also needed to feel him there.

'Let's go and sit down,'said Dad, 'then we can talk.'

They moved across to a corner and sat down on some blankets.

Chapter Four

JIMMY JOINS THE BARTS

'FIRST of all, the house,' said Dad. 'We won't be able to move back for a few days. I'll put a tarpaulin on the roof to keep the rain out, but we won't be able to sleep upstairs for quite a long time — until the roof's repaired.'

'Where shall we sleep then?' asked Fran. Her lip trembled and she looked ready to start crying.

'We'll move the beds downstairs. You'll all have to sleep in the front room and Mum and me in the living room,' said Dad.

'If we keep having raids, we'll either have to improve the shelter, or Aunty Dot says you can all go up there to sleep.'

'What, climb up Hollow Lane *every* night?' asked Bill, sounding incredulous. 'Rather a long way to go to bed.'

'Well — you might be safer up there. There's talk of the ARP making sure that no women and children are sleeping in the town,' said Dad.

'Where will they find beds for everyone?' asked Emma.

'Well, they'll have to sleep in the fields, under the trees and hedges I s'pose,' replied Dad.

'What about Mrs Farmer?' asked Mum.

'Well, she wouldn't listen to me,' said Dad. 'Insisted on climbing over the rubble into her house, knocking the bricks and glass off her armchair and sitting there!'

'But there weren't any lights, were there?' asked Bill.

'No lights, no water and no gas. She wanted a cup of tea and thought I was being awkward when I said it wasn't possible,' Dad answered.

'What happened next?' asked Mum.

'Fortunately, I'd warned Mr King that there might be trouble and he arrived with two other ARP wardens. They didn't give her a chance to say anything. The three of them lifted her up and carried her out,' said Dad with a little smile.

'Then what?' asked Emma.

'The wardens took her up to Mount Fields,' replied Dad.

'The Old People's Home?' questioned Bill.

'Yes,' said Dad. 'Thank goodness they hadn't been hit and had a spare bed.'

'What a relief,' said Mum. 'How long will they keep her?'

'Until her house is ready — and that might take a long time,' said Dad. 'She'll be safer up there, anyway.'

'What will we do for the next few days?' asked Bill, sounding worried.

'Stay here, I'm afraid,' said Dad. 'They'll provide food and everything.'

'What about school?' asked Emma. There were so many questions.

'Your school has gone completely, I'm afraid,' said Dad gently. 'Half of the boys' school is still standing, Bill, so you might go back soon.'

'Can we go down and find out?' asked Bill.

'P'raps — after breakfast,' replied Dad.

'What about me and Jonty?' asked Fran.

'Well, yours is O.K., but the roof of the infants has gone — so Jonty *may* not be able to go,' replied Dad.

'I'll take you two up later, to find out,' said Mum.

'Breakfast — breakfast,' called the tea lady.

'Better join the queue,' said Mum. 'We can carry on talking whilst we eat.'

Breakfast was not too difficult to serve — two pieces of bread each, a small lump of margarine and a spoonful of red jam on a plate. Bovril and tea were ready, so they had soon collected mugs and plates and returned to their corner. They sat in a circle on their blankets and realised that they were hungry. It had been a long, long night.

As they were finishing, Mum said, 'I think we'd better talk about Jimmy.'

'How is he?' asked Dad, sounding very concerned. 'Have you seen him?'

'We've seen him,' said Bill, 'covered in a blanket,' Emma had never seen her brother look so miserable about someone else.

'He did sit up once — and shouted out,' added Emma. 'It was awful. He said, "It's not all over — it's just starting." ' Her voice trailed off.

'He's right,' said Dad slowly. 'It is for him. What are we going to do to help?'

'I had a chat with Mike,' said Mum. 'Jimmy wants to be with him at the moment.'

'Don't blame him,' said Bill. 'Old Mike's a marvellous chap.'

'But he can't stay with Mike for always,' said Mum.

'Mike lives in one room in Mrs Fagg's house. There just isn't room.'

'Where can he go?' asked Emma.

'Well, that's what Mike wanted to chat to me about,' said

Mum. 'He suggests that he brings Jimmy up here today to be with us, for as long as we stay in the old school. I thought,' she went on slowly, 'that we might be able to take him home to live with us after that — but if we've all got to sleep downstairs, I don't know how we'd manage.'

'I'm not sure how we'll manage anyway,' said Dad in a troubled voice. 'The boys share a room — and we've got no bathroom.'

'Neither did the Turners have a bathroom — so he's used to everyone scrambling for the sink in the mornings and having a bath once a week in the kitchen,' said Bill. *That's* not a problem. Anyway, Jonty could sleep in Mum and Dad's room and Jimmy could come in with me.'

'Hey,' said Dad, 'but you two don't always get on.'

'I know,' said Bill, 'but we're not *enemies* — we just have friendly fights! I promise, I really promise, that if he comes to live with us, we will not fight.'

'Hope you can keep that promise,' said Mum doubtfully. 'What do the rest of you think?'

'I think he should come to us,' said Emma firmly.

'And me,' said Fran.

'And me,' piped up Jonty. 'I like Jimmy. He's fun.'

'I don't think he'll be much fun just now,' said Mum gently. 'It'll be a different Jimmy.'

'I know,' said Dad anxiously. 'That's what worries me. We don't know *how* different. But, the Barts have made a decision. Jimmy can live with us — if he wants to.'

Dad took his watch out of his pocket and looked at it.

'Think I'd better be going,' he said.

'But where?' asked Jonty.

'There's lots of work to be done,' replied Dad.

He kissed them all. 'See you soon,' he said and went off through the heavy oak doors. They knew he had a busy day ahead, helping to clear up the bombed houses and shops.

'Hope it won't be *too* dangerous,' thought Emma.

As they sat glumly on the blankets, Mum gathered up the dirty mugs and plates. She took them off into the cloakroom to wash up.

'Dad's on fire-duty all night tonight, isn't he?' said Bill.

'Think so,' said Emma. 'Weren't we lucky that he was with us last night. At least we *knew* he was all right.'

'Hope they don't come back tonight,' went on Bill.

'Why do they *want* to come back here? Why can't they go somewhere else?' blurted out Fran.

'Oh Fran,' said Emma, 'we couldn't want them to go and bomb someone else.'

'Then why don't they *all* stop it?' Fran went on.

'They haven't got the cathedral yet,' said Bill bitterly. 'They'll be back.'

Mum appeared through the door with clean mugs and plates. As she walked towards them, an ARP lady called her back into the cloakroom. A few minutes later, she re-appeared with Jimmy.

He came into the room reluctantly. His head was down, as if he did not want to look at people — did not want to speak to them. He just wanted to be left alone.

Emma and Bill moved up, so that there was space on the blanket. Jimmy plonked himself down, drew up his knees and put his head down.

They all felt awkward — Jimmy was usually so lively, with *too* much to say. Even Mum did not seem quite sure what to do.

'I think it's time we had a hot drink,' she said.

They were about to protest that they had only just had breakfast, when she held up her hand and they knew they

31

had to have another drink, whether they wanted it, or not.

'Come with me, Emma,' she said. 'Help me to carry them.'

The tea lady looked surprised.

'*More* hot drinks?' she exclaimed.

'Well, yes. *We* don't need them, but I'm sure Jimmy does and I've got to get him feeling warm and welcome,' said Mum in a quiet voice.

'Sure. You're right,' said the lady. 'Poor lad.'

They carried the tea and hot Bovril back to their corner and Mum whispered to Emma, 'I want *you* to give one to Jimmy.'

'Me?' Emma looked, and felt, a bit startled. She was not sure that she could get him to look up and take a drink.

'Yes,' said Mum. 'I think he'll take it more easily from you than from the rest of us.'

Emma felt nervous as she sat down next to Jimmy and gently touched his hand.

'Jimmy, would you like a hot drink?' she asked. 'It's hot Bovril.'

Jimmy lifted his face and took the drink from her.

'Thanks Em,' he said.

Silently he sipped it and his face began to relax. He emptied the cup.

'I think I needed that,' he said. 'It's the first drink I've had for hours and hours.'

His face looked very miserable again and they knew he was remembering his last drink — and not wanting to remember — at least, not yet.

'Have another one,' said Bill suddenly.

'O.K.,' said Jimmy — and smiled.

'I'll get it,' said Bill and went over to the tea lady. The rest were still slowly sipping their first cups and Jonty was not sure that he could manage it all.

Bill returned with the drink and was glad to see Jimmy looking part of *his* family.

'We'd better talk about what we are going to do,' Mum said. 'Do we *really* want to stay here all day?'

'Oh no,' they all said — even Jimmy.

'Now, there aren't many choices,' she went on.

'We'll have to come back here for our dinner at mid-day, otherwise we won't get any food. All of your schools have got problems, so the teachers might need some help.'

'Oh yes, we'd like to help,' said Bill, Emma and Jimmy.

'Give us something to do — and stop me thinking,' said Jimmy.

'Don't know what *we* can do,' said Fran. 'Jonty and me are too young to help.'

Just then, Mr King the ARP Warden came through the door and walked towards them, his tin helmet still on his head. When he was not being a warden, he was the School Attendance Officer and rode round the streets on a very large, black bike. He was a large man, with a shock of black hair and a big black moustache. Most of the children were afraid of him and ran if they saw him coming. But he lived near the Bartons and they knew that even if he had a deep, gruff voice, he was quite nice inside, really.

If their ball went into his garden, as long as it did not break any windows, he always threw it back. Not like Fanny Farmer who kept them all! She had *their* balls piled high round her big old mangle*. When Bill and Emma went to do her shopping for her they wanted to pinch the balls back. Once Bill did and Mum and Dad were *very* angry with him.

* Wringer for wet washing.

Now, Mr King was coming towards them. What did he want?

'Oh good,' he said in his deep voice. 'I was hoping to find you all here. Will you help me?'

Would *they* help *him!*

'We'd love to,' they said.

'What can we do?' asked Bill.

'Well, you know that your school has been partly destroyed, and the girls' school is just a heap of rubble?' asked Mr King.

'Yes. Dad told us,' said Emma.

'There were piles of blankets stored in the school to use if we needed them in an air-raid — like you're using these now,' he went on.

'Yes, I saw them,' said Emma, 'piled in the domestic

science block and behind the school hall.'

'And in our school they were at the back of the wood-work room,' said Jimmy. 'Piles and piles of them.'

'Well, the firemen have thrown lots of the blankets out onto the playground, but, they're soaking wet from the firemen's water and covered in dust and rubble,' said Mr King.

'What can *we* do with them?' asked Bill.

'Will you come down with me now to the school, shake them and lay them out flat on the playground?' said Mr King.

'Why lay them out?' asked Emma.

'Well, if it's as hot this week as it was last, the blankets will dry in the hot sun,' said Mr King. 'They may be dirty and smell of burning, but at least we could use them in an emergency. We can't do that now.'

'Will they dry right through?' asked Jimmy.

'No,' replied Mr King. 'You'll need to turn them over in a couple of hours, or so. Will you do it?'

'Yes,' said Bill. 'That's a job we really *can* do.'

'And we'll feel we're doing something to help,' said Emma.

'Much better than just hanging around,' mumbled Jimmy.

'What if there's another raid?' asked Mum anxiously.

'Don't worry,' replied Mr King. 'There'll be plenty of adults around to make sure they go into the shelter — and I'll bring them back here at dinner-time.'

Mum looked relieved.

'That's fine,' she said. 'I'll take Fran and Jonty up to their school.'

Bill, Emma and Jimmy jumped up, waved to Mum and the young ones and followed Mr King out through the door.

Emma thought, 'It's still frightening and sad — but somehow, exciting.'

Chapter Five

RUBBLE, RUBBLE AND MORE RUBBLE

EMMA walked with Mr King and the boys followed behind. They came round by the Dane John and under the bridge, then stopped.

Nothing had prepared them for what they saw now.

Where there had been shops and houses, there were just piles of rubble with a few walls and empty window frames standing eerily erect.

'I don't think I want to look,' murmured Jimmy.

'Come on,' said Bill. 'Keep your eyes down and I'll guide you.'

'Do you still want to go to the school?' he continued carefully.

'Oh yes,' said Jimmy in desperation. 'I must *do* something.'

'O.K. then,' said Bill. 'I'll make sure you get there safely.'

Emma felt proud of her brother. He sounded so grown-up and reassuring. Mr King led her along a wide path between two piles of rubble. She looked around, startled. They were walking towards the back entrance of the school.

'The *back entrance* of the school!' thought Emma, incredulous at the change.

That pile of rubble must have been Moggy Adam's shop.

'Where is Moggy? What about all her cats?' thought Emma.

Mum would not let them buy sweets in Moggy's shop because of the cats. She had about twenty and they slept all over the sweets — on boxes, in the shop window and on the counter. All of the sweets tasted and smelled of cats.

'What's happened to Mog — the lady who had that shop?' Emma asked Mr King quietly, stopping herself *just* in time. She must be careful with him about the nicknames they gave adults.

'The firemen got her out just in time,' replied Mr King. 'She was hiding under the shop counter. It must have been very strong, because it really protected her.'

'Where is she now?' asked Emma.

'They've taken her to Mount Fields,' said Mr King.

'Mount Fields,' Emma gasped. She had a vision of Fanny Farmer and Moggy Adams sharing a room! The poor nurses would have problems. She did not say *this* aloud, instead she asked.

'What about all those cats?'

'They're probably around somewhere searching for food and water,' replied Mr King.

Just then, the boys called out. 'Stop. Can you hear a cat crying?'

Sure enough, from under the piles of rubble, they could hear the desperate cries of a trapped cat. Mr King walked back towards the sound.

'I don't think we can rescue him,' he said. 'We might cause more trouble by trying to shift this rubble.'

He bent down and put his ear to an enormous pile of bricks.

'The cat seems to be trapped behind these,' he said.

'*Can't* we get him out?' asked Jimmy.

''Fraid not,' said Mr King. 'It would be too dangerous.'

The boys looked very disappointed and were reluctant to leave the crying animal. Mr King and Emma walked on up the path and into the boys' playground. Bill and Jimmy followed slowly.

They stopped and looked around. The classrooms to the right were standing and, amazingly, the windows had not been blown out.

'Perhaps it was because of all those wretched brown paper strips we had to lick, and stick over the windows,' thought Emma, remembering the art lesson they had missed to do the job in their classroom — and the revolting taste of the glue.

She then looked beyond the boys' school. The walls of Miss Cannon's study remained. One half of the front door was swinging open — the other half was missing. Behind the gaping door was no neat corridor leading down to the hall, but just piles and piles of broken bricks.

Emma's classroom had been at the back of the hall. She knew it must have gone, because the sky-line beyond the study was empty.

'Awful, isn't it,' said Bill at last.

'Awful,' echoed Jimmy dismally, 'and not just here.'

Emma squeezed his hand and he, to her surprise, squeezed hers back. At least he knew she understood.

'Now, Mr King,' he said. 'Tell us what to do.'

He *had* to start *doing* something.

They followed Mr King across the playground to an enormous grey pile. As they got nearer, they could see that this was a pile of dusty, singed, grey blankets, mixed with bits of brick and glass.

'There they are,' said Mr King. 'I suggest you shake them into the flower bed and then lay them out flat. The sun's coming out and it feels quite warm, so I think we'll be all right. Can you organise yourselves?'

'Oh yes,' said Bill. 'No problem.'

'Right. Then I'll go into the Boys' School,' said Mr King, 'and tell them you're here — just in case there's another raid, or something. I'll be back at about dinner time. Cheerio!'

'Bye,' they said and were just about to start work when Emma said cautiously, 'Do you think we should take our jerseys off first? We're soon not going to need them, because it'll be too hot. If we keep them on, they'll be pretty dirty.'

'You're right,' said Bill.

'What have you got on underneath?' asked Jimmy doubtfully.

Bill stopped and laughed, 'My pyjama jacket! I've only just remembered.'

'Me too,' laughed Emma.

'And me,' joined in Jimmy, looking relieved.

They whipped off their jumpers and got on with the job, Bill fetching the blankets, Emma and Jimmy shaking them, and then laying them out in straight lines.

Soon the boys' playground was full, with just enough room left to walk round the edge.

'Let's go into the girls' playground,' said Bill. Emma and Jimmy followed him through the arch.

'Not sure that we're going to lay many out here,' said Jimmy doubtfully. 'The playground's covered with rubble.'

'What shall we do then?' asked Emma.

'Tell you what, Em,' said Jimmy suddenly, 'you stay here with the blankets and Bill and I'll go back to try and rescue that cat.'

'You can't,' said Emma. 'Mr King said it would be too dangerous.'

'Well, I'd like to try,' said Jimmy. 'Coming Bill?'

41

'If you're going, I'm coming with you,' said Bill.

'O.K. Em?' asked Jimmy.

'O.K.,' said Emma reluctantly.

She watched them dash off through the gates and crouched on a blanket, half-hidden by a tree, hoping that no-one would come and nothing more would happen.

Chapter Six

MOGGY'S CAT CAUSES TROUBLE

'AND *what* are you doing there?' boomed a familiar voice. Emma looked up and saw Duch, her headmistress, glaring down at her. Miss Cannon was known as Duch to countless Blankton old girls, as well as those still at the school.

'Stand up when I speak to you,' went on Duch, looking like a very royal duchess.

Nervously, Emma stood, praying that Duch would not ask too many questions.

'We've — we've been laying out blankets to dry,' she replied. 'Mr King asked us to.' She hoped that Mr King's name would make it all seem 'official'.

'Where, and who, are the others?' asked Duch, relaxing just a little.

'My brother and his friend,' replied Emma.

'Where are they now?' asked Duch, persisting with her questions.

'They'll — they'll be back in a minute,' replied Emma *very* nervously. 'Please let her stop,' she thought.

'Well, they are boys and not my responsibility,' said Duch.

'Mr King is collecting us at dinner-time,' offered Emma, helpfully.

'I'll leave you all to him, today,' said Duch, 'but I expect to see you at school tomorrow.'

'But we — we haven't got a school,' stammered Emma before she could stop herself.

'Teachers and pupils make schools,' said Duch firmly, 'not buildings.'

There was a moment's silence, whilst she let that statement sink in.

'We're sharing what's left of the Boys' School until we can make more permanent arrangements,' said Duch. 'I shall expect to see you at half past eight tomorrow morning, *whatever* happens tonight. Good morning.'

With that, she marched off into the Boys' School and Emma heaved a big sigh of relief to have been let off so lightly. She dropped back onto the blankets to recover.

Seconds later, the wail of the sirens began.

'Oh no,' she thought. 'What can I do? What about the boys? I *wish* they'd come back.'

She sat on, hiding behind the trees. Peeping towards the back gate of the school, *willing* the boys to come.

Still they did not.

'Tug-Boat Annie, please, *please* be quiet,' she pleaded. 'We'll be O.K. if you don't go.'

In the distance she heard gun fire and the drone of planes.

'Not here. Not here,' she prayed.

Whoo-AR! Whoo-AR! WHOO-AR!

The dreaded warning sound of Tug-Boat Annie belched forth.

'What shall I do? Where shall I go?' thought Emma frantically. 'If I go into the school shelter and see Mr King, or someone else from school, they'll ask me where the boys are.'

She clenched her hands, thinking hard.

'If I dash now, I can get to the Dane John shelter — I hope. I'd rather explain to Mum and Old Mike, than to Duch, or Mr King.'

She slipped out from behind the tree and made a dash across the blankets, kicking a few as she ran. She reached the gate and did not look back as she heard the feet of adults running to the school shelter.

The planes were roaring overhead and guns were booming. With her heart in her mouth, she ran round huge piles of rubble, through an alley way, into the Dane John park.

'Please let me get there before anything happens,' she prayed as the bangs got louder and a plane zoomed down.

Was it crashing — or bombing?

Breathless, she reached the shelter door and fell in, just as there was an almighty explosion. She simply collapsed, shaking all over.

'What's up with you, young 'un?' asked a man standing nearby. She was so out of breath, she could not reply. Another loud explosion, followed by another — and, at that moment, the shelter door was flung open.

Two boys tumbled in, Bill and Jimmy.

She cried out, 'You're here! You're here! But where have you been? I've been so worried.'

They picked themselves up and Emma heard a faint miaow coming from inside Jimmy's pyjama jacket. A little furry, ginger face peeped out.

'You got him,' she exclaimed in amazement. 'How did you manage it?'

'It wasn't easy,' said Bill, 'but Jimmy was very brave.'

'It was nothing,' said Jimmy, embarrassed. 'So were you. Come on Em, let's go and find your Mum and Old Mike.'

'Yeah,' replied Emma. 'I think we'll be safer with them, in case Duch, or Mr King ask any questions.

'We can say we wanted to be with Mum and not in the school shelter,' said Bill.

'So that she wouldn't be worried,' went on Emma. 'I don't really like telling fibs though,' she added.

'All in a good cause,' said Jimmy. 'We've saved Ginger's life — so it must be worth it.'

They pushed their way through the benches and knees towards the music. Old Mike was there with his mouth-organ, but no-one much was singing. There was a gloomy atmosphere, as if everyone was too tired to sing.

'Thank goodness for Old Mike,' said Jimmy. 'It'd be awful without him.'

Bill looked around. 'Where's Mum?' he asked in alarm.

'She's not here,' said Emma and suddenly felt *very* frightened.

Mum, Fran and Jonty were *not* here. Where were they?

Those two big explosions meant *something*.

'Oh please, please not them. Don't let anything happen to them. I couldn't stand it,' she thought miserably, as she turned and burried her face on Bill's shoulder. He put his arm round her and gave her a squeeze.

'It'll be all right, Em. It *must* be all right,' he said.

'Let's go and sit by Old Mike,' said Jimmy, feeling desperate. 'Not them too,' he was thinking.

They sat down silently on the bench and Old Mike stopped playing.

'I thought you three were at Blankton School laying out blankets?' he said. 'Why didn't you go to the school shelter?'

Before they could reply, a faint miaow came from Jimmy's pyjama jacket and the little ginger face appeared.

'What on earth have you got there?' exclaimed Old Mike.

'One of Moggy Adam's cats,' replied Jimmy.

'How on earth did you get that?' asked Old Mike.

'It's quite a long story,' replied Bill, 'but Ginger's really the reason why we're here.'

'Do you know where Mum is?' asked Emma in a tiny scared voice.

'Well I *think* she took the other two up to their school. Perhaps she's in the shelter up there,' replied Old Mike, hopefully.

'Do you think so?' asked Bill fervently.

'Hope she wasn't on her way back,' said Emma nervously. 'There aren't really a lot of public shelters between there and the Dane John.'

'No-o,' agreed Old Mike reluctantly.

'And there were two big explosions,' continued Emma.

47

'Now listen, young Emma,' said Old Mike. 'Try not to worry. Let's believe they're all right.'

'Yes,' agreed Jimmy. 'Believe, Em — really hard. I *want* your family to always be here. I've lost mine, but please, *please* let's keep yours.'

He took her hand and gave it a squeeze. Bill was silent, obviously as worried as she was.

Whoo-AR-AR-AR.

Tug-Boat Annie boomed the 'All Clear'.

Bill jumped up.

'I should wait until the siren goes 'All Clear', too,' said Old Mike and gently pulled him back down.

'O.K.,' said Bill reluctantly.

Jimmy lifted Ginger out of his jacket and began to stroke him. Emma stroked too and Ginger began to purr.

'At least *he's* happy,' she thought.

The 'All Clear' sounded and they stood up.

Emma was not sure that she really *wanted* to go out. At least now she could believe that Mum, Fran, Jonty and Dad were safe. If she went outside, someone might tell her that they were not.

Back through the now empty benches they walked to the shelter door.

'Come on,' said Old Mike, 'out you go.'

'I don't want to,' she whispered. 'They may *not* be . . .' Her voice trailed off.

'Come on, Em,' said Bill. 'We'll find out together.'

'Yes,' thought Jimmy. 'You do still have each other.'

They climbed out into the sunlight and saw Dad coming towards them. Emma left Bill and rushed up to him.

'Where are they? Where are they?' she cried.

'They're O.K. It's you we were worried about,' replied Dad.

'Us?' they stammered.

48

'Yes,' said Dad. 'When Tug-Boat Annie went, I was working on a bombed building in the town, so I went into the Blankton School shelter to find you. I spoke to Miss Cannon and Mr King and they both said you'd all disappeared. I couldn't make out where you'd all gone — and I was pretty worried.'

'Sorry, Dad,' mumbled Bill and Emma.

'Sorry. Mr Barton,' said Jimmy, 'we should have been more thoughtful.'

'Yes — you should.' said Dad. 'Quite a lot of people have been worried about you, including Mum.'

'But where *is* Mum?' asked Emma, feeling very upset by this time. She was worried about Mum — and now Dad was cross. What a terrible war it was!

'Mum, Fran and Jonty were in the shelter back home during the raid,' said Dad.

'But what are they doing there?' asked Bill.

'Well, I went up to Winfield School to find them — after I'd lost you,' replied Dad, 'only to be told that they'd left and were on their way back to the old school.'

'Oh, no! Mum, Fran and Jonty walking through all that mess and rubble,' said Bill, 'and Tug-Boat Annie going again.'

'They must have been *really* scared,' said Jimmy.

'Trust Mum to find the answer,' went on Dad. 'They were near our house and she whipped them into the shelter in our own back-yard.'

'But why did you look there?' asked incredulous Emma.

'Well, I stood outside Winfield School and thought — what would I do if I was walking back and Tug-Boat Annie sounded,' replied Dad. 'Go home, of course!'

'I bet Mum was thrilled to see you,' said Bill.

'Yes,' said Dad, 'but worried when I told her that I couldn't find you.'

'We worried about her — and she was worried about us,' said Bill. 'How awful.'

'It's so much better when we're all together. You feel much safer then,' said Emma.

'What about those big explosions?' asked Jimmy.

'They were planes crashing,' replied Dad. 'Actually one came down in a field in Hollow Lane and the other in Thanington, I think.'

'Where's Mum now?' asked Bill.

'Back at the old school,' replied Dad. 'Let's go and find her and have some dinner.'

'Dinner-time. Mr King!' Emma panicked. 'What shall we do?'

'You three go straight back to Mum,' said Dad, 'and I'll go and try to explain some of this to Mr King.'

'Will you, Dad?' asked Bill, sounding relieved.

'Yes, I will,' said Dad. *'But*, after dinner, you must all go and apologise for the worry you've caused.'

'To Mr King?' asked Emma hopefully.

'To Duch *and* Mr King,' said Dad firmly.

Chapter Seven

APOLOGIES TO DUCH

BACK at the old school Emma and the boys happily joined Mum, Fran and Jonty in the queue for dinner. Everyone was relieved to know that the others were safe. Tug-Boat Annie had sounded again. Planes had passed over and some had crashed, but the Barts were *still* together. As she stood in the queue, Emma heaved a big sigh of relief.

'How long's it going on?' she wondered, as she picked up a plate and held it out for a dollop of mashed potatoes, a spoonful of soggy peas, one sausage and some gravy. She picked up a dish of 'sloppy' pudding, not sure whether it was semolina, ground rice, or a greyish sort of custard. She really *hated* 'sloppy' puddings, but knew that she must eat what she was given and say nothing horrid about it. Like school dinners, eating everything and saying nothing, was sometimes not easy.

She tried to eat — not look — imagining that it was something quite different. Since the war had started, there was very little meat, but at home, they had lots and lots of fresh vegetables. Dad had a big allotment near the house and they never seemed to be short of long, scrunchy carrots and jacket potatoes in the winter, then in the summer, there were buckets of peas and beans. They all

51

had to help with weeding and picking, but it was worth it.

The Barts and Jimmy settled themselves in a corner to eat and chat. Just as they finished, Dad came in.

'I've seen Mr King about this morning,' he said. 'Quite honestly he was amazed that you'd got the cat out, but was *very* concerned about the danger. He'll be up here later to have a word with you.'

'What about Duch?' asked Emma fearfully.

'I didn't see her and Mr King says she's pretty busy sorting out school premises and everything. He suggests you write to her.'

'Oh flip!' said Bill. 'Writing a letter to *her* might be even worse than seeing her.'

'Maybe — but you've got to do it, so I suggest you go off and start now,' said Dad.

'We haven't any paper and pencil,' said Emma hopefully. If they had not the tools, they could not do the job.

'Mr King thought of that,' said Dad and produced paper, envelope and pencil from his pocket.

The boys groaned.

'We've got no excuse then,' said Bill with a sigh. 'Come on you two.'

'Mrs Bart,' said Jimmy, 'could you take Ginger and see if there are any scraps for him?'

'Oh, yes,' said Fran. 'We'll look after Ginger, won't we Jonty?'

'Mm,' said Jonty, his face beaming.

Jimmy lifted Ginger out of his pyjama jacket, handed him to Fran and followed Emma and Bill across the room to a far corner.

'Now Em,' Bill was saying. 'She's your head mistress, so you'd better do the writing.'

'Oh no,' protested Emma. 'You're both older than me,

52

can't one of you?' She certainly did not want to write to Duch.

She stopped when she saw Bill's face, *pleading* with her to agree. Then she understood, more clearly than ever before. Bill was *afraid* to write the letter. He could not spell, and as soon as he wrote anything down, he told the world about his difficulties.

Perhaps even Jimmy did not know and Emma saw that she had to help Bill keep his secret.

'O.K. I'll write it,' she said. 'You tell me what to say.'

Bill's face relaxed. He had ideas — it was just getting them down on paper that bothered him.

'Well,' he started, 'we must be very polite and apologetic.'

They discussed exactly what to say, before Emma began to write. Half an hour later, the letter was finished.

Dear Miss Cannon,

Please forgive us for behaving so thoughtlessly this morning.

We wanted to save the life of a cat and forgot the adults who would wurry about us, when the siren and Tug-Boat Annie went.

We know that you are very busy sorting out the school and are sorry that we were not helpful in the way we behaved.

Yours sincerely
Emma Barton,
James Turner
and William Barton.

The boys signed their names and read through the finished letter.

'Sounds good to me,' said Jimmy. 'You write jolly well, Em. Better than me.'

'Mm — better than me, too,' mumbled Bill.

'Better let Mum see it,' said Emma, 'in case some of my spellings are wrong.'

'*Your* spellings are *good*,' said Bill. 'Bet she doesn't find any mistakes.'

'Well, I want her to see it just the same,' said Emma firmly, anxious that the letter should be perfect.

Mum read the letter. 'Very good,' she said. 'That's a nice letter — even Duch must forgive you after that.'

'Are all my spellings right?' asked Emma anxiously.

'Well, there are a couple of mistakes, but you can put them right easily,' she said.

'What are they?' Emma peered over at the letter again.

'First of all — "worry",' said Mum. 'It's an odd word.

You've written it as it sounds. All you've got to do is to change the "u" into "o".'

Carefully, very carefully, Emma changed the letter.

'Anything else?' she queried.

'One more,' Mum said. 'Sincerely is a funny word too. You have to remember *all* of the bits — sin-ce-re-ly. You've got room to squeeze an extra "e" after the "r".'

Emma carefully wrote it in.

'I never knew that,' said Jimmy. 'Now I'll remember it — all the bits! Wonder how many times I've written that wrongly. But then, I don't have to write many letters and those I do write, usually end in "Love from".'

Emma put the letter into the envelope and addressed it to Miss Cannon.

One of the ARP ladies came towards them.

'Will you be staying here tonight, Mrs Barton?' she asked.

'I think we'll have to,' said Mum. 'We can't go back into the house and we haven't had a chance to sort anything else out.' Mum looked worried.

'No problem,' said the ARP lady. 'You'll find a corner somewhere. Let's hope we can sleep tonight. I'm sure we need it.'

'Mr King's just arrived,' called Bill.

'Wonder what he'll say,' said Jimmy to Emma.

Mr King's tall figure came towards them.

'You got it then,' he said to Jimmy and Bill.

'Yes, we got it,' said Bill cautiously.

'You saved one cat — and caused us all a lot of worry. Never do that again,' Mr King said firmly. 'Do you understand?'

'Yes, Mr King,' said Bill looking subdued.

'Sorry Mr King,' said Jimmy.

'We've written a letter to Miss Cannon,' said Emma 'to

say we're sorry. Will you give it to her?'

'Yes, I will,' he said.

'Now you'd better come with me to turn over those blankets — and remember, you *stay* there. If the siren goes, you go straight into the Blankton shelters — and nowhere else. That's right isn't it Mrs Barton?'

'Yes — absolutely,' said Mum. 'They're really very sorry and I'm sure they'll not disappear this afternoon. See you all at tea-time.'

'Fran, can I leave Ginger with you?' asked Jimmy.

Fran beamed. 'I'd love to have him,' she said.

'And me — and me,' put in Jonty.

'O.K. — and you,' laughed Jimmy.

'It's good to see Jimmy laugh,' thought Emma.

Chapter Eight

THE MANGLED WHALE

THE blankets had dried well in the hot sun and speedily they turned them over.

'I wonder if there's anything we can do to clear up the girls' playground and put some more out there,' said Bill.

'Let's look,' Jimmy said and they all walked across to the arch, then stopped in amazement. A large lorry stood in the middle of the playground and the rubble was piled in huge mounds at the far side.

Airmen, in blue shirts and trousers were pulling a large, grey, floppy thing across the cleared spaces.

'What on earth's that?' asked Emma, sounding puzzled.

'Dunno,' said Bill, equally puzzled.

They watched as the airmen stretched the grey thing out flat.

'Looks like a mangled whale,' muttered Jimmy.

A noise startled them! As the noise continued, the 'mangled whale' grew. It grew and grew until it was an enormous air-balloon. Watching with amazement they saw the 'whale' begin to rise from the ground, into the air.

Emma looked around the sky and could see other grey whales rising all over the city.

'What on earth are they for?' exclaimed Bill as he spotted them.

At this point, the busy airmen relaxed. The job of getting the balloon into the air was over.

'Tea-up,' a voice called and the men walked towards a tent.

One of them turned and saw the three teenagers standing between the two playgrounds.

'Hi! — what are you doing here?' he called.

'Putting out blankets,' replied Bill.

'Why? Are you going to sleep here?' the airman laughed as he walked towards them. He looked into the other playground.

'Coo. That was a dusty job,' he said.

'We've just finished turning them over,' said Jimmy.

'Come and have a mug of tea with us,' said the airman and took them towards the tent.

Bill could see three stripes on his blue shirt — and knew

he must be important. When he reached the tent, he called out. 'Out of the way, you chaps. Tea for the workers.'

The airmen looked round, 'Hi,' they said.

'Hi, Hi,' said Bill, Jimmy and Emma, excited at being welcomed into the tent.

The 'striped' airman called, 'Do you all take sugar?'

'Please,' they said, and he brought the tea over to them.

It was *very* strong. 'Looks more like Bovril than tea!' thought Emma, glad that she'd asked for sugar.

'What's the big air balloon for?' asked Bill. 'We haven't had any here before.'

'No,' said the 'striped' airman. 'You probably should have. It's a barrage balloon. There are quite a lot in and around the city now. The idea is that the aircraft will not be able to dive-bomb the buildings.'

'We should be safer then,' commented Bill.

'Yep — we all hope so,' replied the airman. 'Come over and meet the others.'

He took them to a group who were laughing and talking whilst they drank their tea.

'Meet the "blanket kids",' he said. 'What are your names?'

'Emma.'

'Bill.' ·

'Jimmy,' they replied.

One of the airmen, who seemed slightly older than the rest, was looking hard at Jimmy.

'Do any of you know the Turner family?' he asked.

Jimmy's face crumpled — he could *not* reply.

Bill said quietly, 'Yes. They were all great friends of ours.'

At that, Jimmy rushed from the tent. He could not stand there and talk about his family.

'Shall I follow him?' asked Emma, very upset at Jimmy's distress.

'Wait a bit,' said Bill. He turned to the airman. 'That's Jimmy Turner. The rest of his family were all killed last night.'

The airman looked shocked and upset. 'How could I?' he said. 'Fancy asking *that* question today of all days. Somehow, I hadn't thought of anyone I *knew* being killed.'

'Do you know the Turners then?' asked Bill.

'Yes,' said the airman. 'I'm Jimmy's uncle. I was only posted here today. Thought it would be good to see my brother and his family again.' His voice trailed off. He was obviously very upset.

'I'm not sure what to do,' he went on, sounding troubled. 'I don't know Jimmy very well, as we live too far away in Yorkshire, for visits.'

'I knew Jimmy's Dad came from Yorkshire,' said Bill. 'That's why he was so keen on the band. We'll miss him.' He turned and looked at Emma.

'Will you go and see if Jimmy is in the boys' playground?'

'Will he want me?' asked Emma, slightly nervous about Jimmy's reaction.

'I think he'd rather have you than me,' said Bill, reassuringly.

Slowly Emma walked towards the arch, not sure whether she was going to find Jimmy — and if she did, simply not knowing what she could say.

She stood and looked towards the trees where she had crouched whilst waiting for the boys. Sure enough, Jimmy was there, his knees and shoulders hunched together and his head down. She went up and sat on the ground beside him. Gently she put her hand on his shoulder.

'I'm so sorry, Jimmy, about that,' she said. 'It must have been awful.'

'It was,' he replied. 'Terrible. I couldn't stay there and say anything.'

'I think you're going to feel like that for a long, long time Jimmy,' she said. 'I know *I* would.'

'Thanks for coming to find me Em,' he said. 'It helps.' He stood up. 'Shall we go back?'

'If *you* want to,' Emma replied.

Suddenly Jimmy turned. 'Who *is* that chap?' he asked, remembering what had sparked off his distress.

'Your uncle from Yorkshire,' she said.

'Uncle Charlie — Dad's brother?' Jimmy was obviously amazed. 'Fancy him being here today, of *all* days.'

'Yes,' said Emma. 'He's just been posted here and was looking forward to seeing you all.'

'He must be feeling shocked too,' commented Jimmy slowly. 'Let's go back and find him.'

Back in the tent, Bill and Uncle Charlie were now standing apart from the other airmen.

'Hello, old lad,' said Uncle Charlie to Jimmy and held out his hand.

'If you two want to go off for a chat,' said Bill, 'we'll sort out the blankets.'

'Would you like that Jimmy?' his uncle asked. Jimmy nodded and the two walked off together.

'We won't be far away,' Uncle Charlie turned and said.

'And if the siren goes,' said Jimmy, looking more relaxed, 'I promise I'll come straight back. Can't upset Duch and Mr King again.'

'Bye,' said Emma.

'See you later,' said Bill.

'Blankets,' they both said together. They thanked the

'striped' airman for the tea and returned to the boys' playground.

'He's a nice chap,' said Bill, as they started folding the now-dry blankets and stacking them into a neat pile. 'Be good for Jimmy.'

'Did he say anything about any more relations?' asked Emma. 'None of us really thought about them, did we?'

'Yes,' replied Bill. 'He said he must get a message to Jimmy's Grandma in Yorkshire.'

'Has Uncle Charlie got any children?' asked Emma.

'Yes, but they're younger,' said Bill. 'About Fran and Jonty's age, I should think.'

'Could be good for Jimmy to know he's still got a family — somewhere,' said Emma, thoughtfully.

They continued shaking, folding, stacking and were quiet for a bit.

Then Bill said, 'Jimmy's uncle said something about the funeral. Came as a bit of a shock. Hadn't thought about that — and I don't think Jimmy had either.'

'Would he have to go?' asked Emma, thinking how terrible it would be for him.

'I *suppose* so,' said Bill. 'He'd probably feel he'd *got* to go.'

'I'm glad his uncle's here,' said Emma. 'That'll make it easier for him.'

They finished folding and stacking and sat down to wait, still thinking about Jimmy, but not talking.

Emma looked up to see Mr King and Duch coming across the playground towards them. She pulled Bill's pyjama jacket.

'Look,' she whispered and stood up.

He looked up and joined her.

'Only two of you?' questioned Mr King. 'Where's the cat rescuer gone?'

Bill explained about the airmen and Jimmy's uncle.

Mr King was nodding and his face looked relieved.

'I'm glad for the boy,' he said. 'What a miracle!'

He continued, 'Perhaps Jimmy will be able to go to Yorkshire to live with his relations.'

Emma felt a slight shock. She was expecting Jimmy to live with them — and was looking forward to it.

'That would be a very good idea,' said Duch, 'if they can have him.'

She turned to Emma and Bill and, to Emma's surprise, she actually smiled.

'Thank you for your letter,' she said. 'I hope the cat will be very happy with you.'

'Goodbye, Mr King,' she continued. They shook hands and she returned to the school.

'Now, do you want to go back for your tea?' Mr King asked Emma and Bill.

'What about Jimmy?' asked Emma.

'I'll go and have a look — see if he's coming,' said Bill. As he went towards the arch, Jimmy and his uncle appeared.

'I've been to ask the sergeant if I can come back to the old school with you and see your parents,' said Uncle Charlie.

'Well, Mum should be there,' replied Bill. 'Don't know about Dad.'

Then he remembered. 'Oh, Mr King, this is Jimmy's uncle.'

The two men shook hands and they all turned to walk out of the back entrance. Bill, Emma and Jimmy went on ahead.

'I'd forgotten about Grandma,' said Jimmy, in a low voice. 'I shouldn't have forgotten, but I've hardly ever seen her. Yorkshire's so far away. We could never afford the train fares to go up there — and she couldn't afford to

63

come down. Dad and she used to write to each other.'

'When did you last see her?' asked Emma.

'I suppose when I was about five,' said Jimmy. 'Dad came down here to get a job. We all said goodbye — and that was it. We never went back.'

'Do you remember much about Yorkshire?' asked Bill.

'Well, no,' replied Jimmy. 'Only that we seemed to have lots of friends and relations up there — it was fun. When we came down here, we had no-one.'

'I expect your Mum and Dad were lonely,' said Emma.

'Yeah,' said Jimmy. 'It was better when Dad joined the band — and I started to learn the cornet. Then we had real friends again — the Barts for instance,' he added with a grin.

'Yes,' said Bill. 'Our Mums became friends and that must have helped.'

'It did,' agreed Jimmy. 'There was always something happening — people around.'

They reached the old school and stood waiting for Mr King and Uncle Charlie to catch up.

Chapter Nine

UNCLE CHARLIE MEETS THE BARTS

As THEY climbed up the slope to the door, a fluffy little ginger thing rushed out. Fran and Jonty were close behind.

'Come back, Ginger,' shouted Fran.

Jimmy dived forward and caught him. 'You rascal,' he said. 'We didn't rescue you, so that you could get lost.'

He tucked the cat back inside his pyjama jacket and they went inside. Mum was helping the ARP ladies to prepare piles of sandwiches for tea. She turned her head as she heard them come.

'We've got a visitor, I see,' she said.

'It's my Uncle Charlie,' explained Jimmy. 'We met him in the school playground.'

'I've just been posted here,' said Uncle Charlie, as he joined them at the table. 'I still can't believe that all this has happened since four o'clock this morning, when we were ordered to bring the balloon here.'

'I'm glad for Jimmy,' said Mum. 'I know a bit about you and your family. We used to talk, you know. But somehow, I'd forgotten. There've been so many things to worry about in the last few hours.'

'I know,' said Uncle Charlie. 'Why should you think

about us? I'm just so grateful you thought about Jimmy — he is the important one. When will your husband be back?'

'I'm not sure,' said Mum. 'He was hoping to go home after work, get the children some clean clothes and bring them here. He's on duty tonight.'

She looked at her watch. 'He *could* be here in about half an hour. Do you want to wait and have some tea with us?' She looked at the ARP ladies. 'Will that be O.K.?'

They nodded.

'A cup of tea will be fine,' said Uncle Charlie. 'I'll have a meal at the base, later.'

Mum took him across to 'their' corner and they sat down on the blankets. Soon Jimmy and the others were playing around with Ginger, so Mum and Uncle Charlie had time to talk.

'Have you been able to get in touch with the family?' Mum asked.

'Well, no,' replied Uncle Charlie. 'That's one reason why I'd like to speak to your husband. He might be able to tell me how to get a message through.'

'Do you know anyone with a telephone?' asked Mum. 'It'd be quicker than a telegram.' Not many people had telephones at home and Mum did not think that Uncle Charlie's family would be among the lucky ones.

'The minister of our church has got one,' he said thoughtfully. 'I've got the number. Perhaps the police could help me get a message through to him.'

'That would be best,' said Mum. 'He could break the news to your mother in a much kinder way than if a stranger knocked at the door.'

'Has anything been done about the funeral?' asked Uncle Charlie.

'Not that I know of,' said Mum. 'There were so many

people killed and injured last night. I think, at the moment, everybody's concentrating on those still here and *their* problems.'

'I'm sure,' said Uncle Charlie. 'I might be able to make the arrangements — that would help.'

'Will you have time?' asked Mum.

'I've been thinking about that,' replied Uncle Charlie. 'I'm sure the officer would give me compassionate leave — our C.O.'s a very nice chap. Then I could arrange the funeral and perhaps take Jimmy up to Yorkshire to stay with the family.'

'Have you spoken to Jimmy?' asked Mum. 'It sounds a good idea to me.'

'No,' said Uncle Charlie. 'Not yet. It didn't seem right to talk about it just yet.'

'We had thought that Jimmy could come and live with us,' said Mum. 'Our families have been good friends for years, but I'm sure his own family would be better for him — if *he's* happy.'

'I'll talk to him,' said Uncle Charlie. 'Perhaps tomorrow.'

'Dad's here,' called Emma from the door.

'Tea-up,' said the ARP lady.

With Dad *and* tea, the serious talking had to stop. In due course, they sat in a circle with sandwiches and mugs of tea to catch up with Dad's news.

'He looks very tired,' thought Emma.

'What sort of a day has it been?' asked Mum.

'Pretty awful,' replied Dad and looked sad, which was unusual. Dad had a happy, smiling face, which made everyone feel good in his company.

'Did you go into our house?' asked Bill.

'Yes — and I got your school clothes, so you can look respectable tomorrow,' replied Dad.

'Are they clean?' asked Mum anxiously.

'Yes — they seem clean to me,' said Dad. 'The dust and soot doesn't seem to have got into the drawers and cupboards upstairs. The house is a mess and I haven't time to do anything yet about the roof. Probably have to wait 'til the weekend.'

'Hope there are no more raids before then,' muttered Bill.

'How long will we have to stay here?' asked Mum, looking very concerned.

'At least another couple of days — maybe much longer,' said Dad.

'We'll manage,' said Mum with a smile, seeing how tired and worried he looked.

She went on, 'I was talking to the ARP ladies. They say it might be an idea to go into the Dane John shelter at the children's bedtime, so that they can have an uninterrupted night — hopefully.'

'Are there bunks?' asked Emma.

'Yes,' said Mum. 'At one end there're bunks and we can take blankets from here.'

'Sounds a good idea,' said Dad. 'And if you three are going to school tomorrow, you'll need some sleep.'

'Not sure what we'll do at school,' said Jimmy. 'It's all such a mess.'

'We haven't actually *got* a school,' said Emma.

Uncle Charlie turned to Dad. 'Can we have a chat?' he asked.

Jimmy gave them both a quick look, but did not say anything. He knew it must be something to do with him, but at this moment, he just did not want to ask any questions — and certainly did not want to be asked any.

The two men strolled out of the door, whilst Mum and Emma collected the cups.

'We'd better look at the clothes Dad brought,' said Mum. 'I'm not sure what he'll have chosen for you,' she grinned.

'Be glad to get out of my pyjamas,' said Emma. 'Been in them a long time now.'

Mum and Emma sorted out the clothes into separate piles.

'I'm glad Dad's brought some of Bill's clothes for Jimmy,' Emma said.

'The boys are about the same size,' said Mum, 'so they'll fit. I'm not sure that Jimmy has any of his clothes left. The house was completely demolished.' Mum paused. 'But I'm not sure how long we'll be able to last, with one set of clothes between two of them.'

Emma had been checking her things.

'Has he remembered everything?' asked Mum.

'Well, he's brought me long, brown socks instead of short white ones — and no garters*!' said Emma.

'They'll do for tomorrow and we'll have to see if we can get a couple of bits of string to keep your socks up,' said Mum.

'Yes — no-one's going to have any elastic,' said Emma, 'and I *hate* my socks drooping round my ankles. P'raps lots of girls will look a mess tomorrow.'

Dad and Uncle Charlie came back in.

'Where's Jimmy?' asked Dad.

'Chasing Ginger with the others,' said Mum.

'Go and find him, will you Emma love?' Dad asked. 'Don't hurry.'

She went off, knowing that the grown-ups wanted a few moments alone. Outside, she wandered round to the back of the old school and spotted the others at the bottom of the bank.

* Elastic bands to keep socks up.

She called to Jimmy, 'Your Uncle Charlie would like to talk to you.' He scrambled up the bank and walked reluctantly back into the school. Emma watched. His shoulders drooped and his legs moved heavily. He knew what they wanted to talk about — and it was going to be so hard.

'What do they want him for?' asked Bill, as she ran down the bank to them.

'I think to talk about the funeral — and perhaps whether he wants to go and live in Yorkshire with his Gran,' replied Emma.

'Jimmy's only said one thing to me about the funeral,' said Bill.

'What's that?' asked Emma.

'Did I think the band could play,' replied Bill. 'Then he could have his cornet with him. Give him something to *do* and hold on to, he said.'

'Yeah, he's right,' said Emma thoughtfully. 'Jimmy *needs* something to do — he can't just think — it hurts too much. What did you say?'

'Thought it would be a good idea,' said Bill. 'I know his Mum and Dad would have wanted it. They were very proud when Jimmy became solo cornet.'

'I think I'll offer to look after Fran and Jonty, so that Mum can go,' said Emma. 'You'll be all right — you'll have your trombone.'

'See what happens,' said Bill. 'The grown-ups will decide.'

It was quite a long time before Mum came to fetch them.

'Come and say good-night to Dad,' she said. 'Then we're going to the shelter.'

'Do we *have* to?' protested Bill. 'It's not dark yet and the siren hasn't gone for ages.'

'Yes you do,' said Mum firmly. 'It's school tomorrow and you had almost no sleep last night.'

'Is Jimmy coming?' asked Emma.

'Yes,' said Mum. 'He's a bit upset. We've talked about a lot of things and Charlie's gone off to make arrangements for leave. Then he'll organise everything.'

'*Is* Jimmy going to live in Yorkshire?' asked Emma.

'He's thinking about it,' replied Mum. 'Pick up Ginger and let's go.'

As they reached the door the siren began to wail. Some people were already dashing out, but the Barts pushed their way in to say goodbye to Dad, find Jimmy and collect blankets.

Soon they were rushing towards the Dane John, hoping they would reach the shelter before Tug-Boat Annie sounded. She bellowed forth, just as they reached the door. The planes droned overhead, but they seemed further away — not as if they were going to zoom down at any moment.

'Must be those grey 'whales' keeping them out,' said Emma.

'Never thought 'whales' could be so useful,' said Bill.

'Pity they didn't come before,' muttered Jimmy.

Once inside, Mum guided them down towards the bunks.

'Can't we go and see Old Mike?' asked Emma.

'Please,' said Bill, 'just for a little while.'

'Please, Mrs Barton,' joined in Jimmy. 'I'd like to let him see Ginger again.' The cat was, by now, nestling again inside Jimmy's pyjama jacket.

Mum relented at that. 'O.K.,' she said. 'Half-an-hour. That's all. If you're not back, I'll come and fetch you.'

They dumped their blankets on the hard bunks, the boys' on top, Emma's beneath, and dashed off.

Emma knocked her leg on the corner of a bench, the edges were not protected by as many knees tonight.

She wondered why.

'Where is everybody?' she asked.

'Remember Dad said lots of people were going out to sleep in the country,' said Bill. 'I can just imagine them streaming up Hollow Lane and finding a hedge or tree to sleep under.'

'Hope it doesn't rain,' said Emma.

'Better be wet than dead,' said Jimmy, in barely more than a whisper. His face was looking sad and tired since his talk with the grown-ups.

Fortunately, the sound of Old Mike's mouth-organ reached them as they went round the next corner. A few children were with him, but no-one was singing.

'Worn out, like me,' thought Emma.

'Hello, you three,' called Old Mike. 'Nice to see you.'

They sat beside him and Jimmy said, 'Look, there are four of us.'

He opened his pyjama jacket and out peeped a little ginger face.

'Like him?' Jimmy asked.

'Lovely,' said Old Mike. 'You were brave boys to rescue him — and you were a brave girl, Emma, when Duch wanted to know where they were.'

Jimmy lifted Ginger out and Mike stroked him.

'What's this about your uncle from Yorkshire?' he asked.

'Yes,' replied Jimmy. 'Isn't it amazing that he's here as a whale-keeper.'

'A whale-keeper?' Old Mike looked puzzled.

'Those barrage balloons look just like huge whales when they're on the ground,' explained Bill.

'How did you know about Jimmy's uncle?' asked Emma.

'Met Mr King,' said Old Mike.

'Can I ask you something, Mike?' said Jimmy. 'When you're in trouble, who's more important, friends — or relations?'

'That's a hard one, lad,' replied Mike. 'Depends on the friends — and depends on the relations. Sometimes your relations can be your best friends.'

'I wonder . . .' said Jimmy and trailed off.

'What do you wonder?' asked Mike. Emma knew and was anxious to hear what Jimmy would say.

'Well, Uncle Charlie has suggested I could go and live in Yorkshire with his family and my Gran. He's said he'll get leave and take me up after the funeral.' Jimmy stopped abruptly.

'Poor Jimmy,' thought Emma. 'So much to worry him. First the funeral and *then* where to live. I don't think I could cope with all that. I'd just be crying all the time.'

She looked across at Jimmy. If he went to Yorkshire, would she ever see him again? It was such a long way — and cost so much on the train.

'How long ago since you saw your relations?' asked Mike.

'Well, nearly nine years. I was only five,' replied Jimmy.

'I certainly loved them then. My Gran was marvellous — warm and cuddly. Made lovely treacle puddings.'

'What about cousins?' asked Mike.

'They were only babies, so I didn't know them as people,' said Jimmy. 'Could be like having a young brother and sister — again.' He finished the sentence slowly.

'You know,' said Mike gently, 'if you stay here, you're going to be surrounded by memories. Some very happy —

73

and some very, very sad. Might be a good idea to go up there until after the war. Then, if you want to, come back down here again.'

'You can always stay with us,' Emma put in, timidly.

Jimmy looked at her. 'I'll miss the Barts, you know. But p'rhaps I'd better go to Yorkshire.'

'Sleep on it, lad,' said Mike. 'You don't have to decide right now.'

'Have we been here half an hour?' asked Bill.

'Almost,' said Mike. 'One song and then off you go.'

> 'There's a long, long worm a-crawling,
> Across the roof of my tent,
> I can hear the whistle blowing,
> And it's time I went . . .'

He began playing and they all joined in.

'Right,' he said, when they'd finished, 'I can hear your Mum's whistle blowing. Off you go.'

As they crept back through the gloomy passages, the planes droned steadily overhead and they could hear distant gun-fire.

'Not us tonight,' thought Emma.

'Wonder who's going to catch it now?' said Bill.

The benches were fuller and they bumped against strange knees as they wormed their way through.

'Well done,' said Mum in a whisper, as they rounded yet another corner to the bunks.

'Fran and Jonty are asleep,' she went on. 'Come on. Snuggle down all of you. I'm ready for bed too.'

Soon they were all fast asleep, except Jimmy.

'Yorkshire — or Kent?' The question would not leave him. As he finally went to sleep, he tried to picture the stone cottage where his Grandma lived. He remembered the warmth coming from her fire in the living room and the smell of lovely Sunday dinners wafting out of the oven. He

heard Grandma's happy chuckle and thought, 'Perhaps —
perhaps.'

Chapter Ten

BACK AT THE BOMBED SCHOOL

EMMA felt Mum shaking her.

'Time to get up,' she was saying. Emma sat up with a start. The others were still fast asleep. She could see the little ones on their bunks and hear Bill and Jimmy snoring.

'What's the time?' she asked. 'Has the "All Clear" gone?'

'Yes, ages ago,' said Mum, 'and it's now about seven o'clock.'

'Were there any loud explosions in the night?' asked Emma.

'No — not here,' replied Mum. 'I heard the planes go over again — then the "All Clear", so I knew they'd left us alone.'

'I wonder where they've been with those awful bombs,' pondered Emma.

'That's what I wondered too,' said Mum. 'Anyway, get up.' She began to shake the boys.

They bundled up their blankets and crept out of the deserted shelter. It felt even darker and dirtier when the benches were empty. Soon they were at the old school and found some different ARP ladies preparing breakfast.

'Bet the others were tired,' thought Emma.

'Hello, Mrs Bart,' said one. 'Your husband's been in. Said he'd be back for breakfast about half past seven. They'd a quiet night at the fire station.'

'So he's been able to get some sleep, I hope,' said Mum.

'Yes, he looked like his cheerful self — but a bit bristly,' said the ARP lady. 'Said something about going home for a wash and a shave.'

'Is there any water up there?' asked Mum.

'Yes, there's water, but no gas and no electricity,' replied the ARP lady, 'so it'll be a cold wash and shave.'

'Talking of washing,' said Mum. 'Is there somewhere that these youngsters can go for a wash, before school?'

'Yes — in the cloakroom,' replied the ARP lady. 'It's a bit public there, but there's nowhere else. Have you got a towel?'

'Heavens — no!' said Mum, putting her hand over her mouth. 'I forgot that.'

'Well, they can't drip-dry,' laughed the ARP lady. 'Look, I brought a pile of tea towels for the washing up. I can only spare one — so they'll have to share it.'

'Better than nothing,' said Mum, looking relieved. 'Hands and face only, I think.'

Jimmy lifted Ginger out from his pyjama jacket and handed him to Fran.

'Off you go, you three,' Mum went on. 'A lick and a promise.'

'May not be able to keep the promise for a few days,' said the ARP lady, as the three went off. 'No place here for a strip-wash.'

They were back soon, with shining faces, clean hands and one soggy tea towel. Before Jimmy could take Ginger again, they had their next instructions.

'Now, grab your school clothes and find a corner to change in,' said Mum, determined to get them ready for school as quickly as possible.

Emma dashed behind one high pile of desks and the boys behind another. As she put her school dress on, she realised that Dad had brought one she had grown out of. Mum was saving it for Fran. It was *much* too short.

'Thank goodness there isn't a mirror,' she thought. 'At least I don't know how awful I look, with my dress up to my thighs and long, brown socks that are going to slip down because I've got no garters.'

She gathered her dirty clothes from the floor and crept out from behind the desks. She could feel lots of eyes turned towards her.

'Oh dear. I must look terrible,' she thought. 'No-one's laughing though. P'raps they will at school!' She began to dread going.

The boys appeared and both looked pretty normal.

They stared at her and Bill laughed.

'Em, you can't go like that!'

She felt her face go hot and red.

'I know,' she said desperately. 'But what can I *do*?'

'Tell you what, Em,' said Jimmy. 'Take off your socks. Tell them your Dad forgot to bring them.'

'White lie — but worth it,' said Bill.

Emma went back behind the desks and pulled off the socks.

'Thank goodness for the boys,' she thought. 'Better to have long, skinny legs, than droopy, brown socks with a mini, summer dress.'

She reappeared and was greeted by cheers from the boys.

'Come on, you three,' called Mum. 'Breakfast.'

They gathered their mugs of steaming tea, bread,

margarine and red jam. Dad had not appeared yet and so they sat on the blankets in the corner, eating and drinking. As they finished, he poked his head round the door. They could tell he had shaved. Not only had the bristles gone, but he had quite a few little razor cuts on his chin.

'Phew, that was a hard shave,' he said to Mum. 'My tough bristles don't like cold water — and there was two days' growth! That'll teach me a lesson.'

He joined them on the floor, whilst Mum collected his breakfast. Ginger was sitting on the blanket in the middle of the group.

'Any news on the house?' asked Bill.

'Well, I hope I'll be able to get some tarpaulins today and start on it tonight,' replied Dad. 'Then perhaps, if Fran and Jonty are at school tomorrow, Mum could start cleaning up downstairs.'

'So, another couple of days?' questioned Bill.

'Think so,' said Dad. He looked at his watch. 'You three had better start going off to school. Do you want me to come?'

'Oh, no,' said Bill. 'We'll manage.'

'Well, make sure that Emma finds out where she's to go,' said Dad, 'because there's *nothing* of her school left.'

'Don't worry, Mr Bart,' said Jimmy. 'We'll look after her.'

Emma felt warm inside. Jimmy was being *really* nice to her.

He handed Ginger to Fran, 'You look after him,' he said. Fran was delighted.

They waved goodbye and went off.

'You may have to come back here at dinner-time,' called Mum, as they went out of the door. 'School kitchens may be damaged.'

'O.K.' called Bill. 'See you.'

They walked by the Dane John towards the back entrance of Blankton Boys'.

'There's Moggy's shop,' said Emma.

'Let's go and see if there are any more cats,' urged Jimmy.

'Hi, we'd better not crawl around in there today,' said Bill. 'It got us into enough trouble yesterday!'

Jimmy bent his ear down to the rubble.

'Can't hear anything,' he said. 'Not even the faintest sound.'

Emma was relieved. She had been afraid that he would

80

not be able to resist another rescue bid.

They walked through the school gate into the boys' playground. It was full of boys *and* girls.

'The "whale catchers" are in ours,' said Emma.

'Not just the catchers,' said Bill, 'but the whale.'

Over the top of the wall, they could see the huge, grey shape of the barrage balloon.

Emma looked into the sky and, to her surprise, it was empty.

Jimmy saw her look. 'The bombers won't come in the daylight,' he said.

'Hope not,' said Emma. She turned her head and saw a line of twenty, skinny cats parading up the road behind them.

'Moggy's cats!' she exclaimed.

'Where have they come from?' asked Bill. 'And where are they going to?'

'Let's see,' said Jimmy.

They stood and watched the cats walk straight by them, round the playground and through the arch into the girls' playground.

'I know where they're going,' Bill sounded excited.

'Those airmen are feeding them!' said Jimmy.

They all burst out laughing.

'Hi, Bill,' called Tommy North. He came across to where they were standing. 'Hello, Jim,' he said quietly.

Emma knew he must have heard about Jimmy's family and did not know what else to say. There was an awkward silence.

'I must get them talking normally,' she thought desperately.

'Think I'd better go and find the girls,' she said at last. 'You don't know what we're supposed to be doing, Tommy, do you?' His sister was at her school.

'No,' he said, looking relieved. 'Nothing's been said and everyone's just waiting around for the whistle.'

'Can't think where they're going to put us all,' said Jimmy. His face had relaxed again. Emma had watched it tighten when Tommy approached. She knew he did not *want* sympathetic words spoken. He could *feel* genuine sympathy — but could not talk about his family.

'There's Audrey,' said Tommy, as his sister walked towards them. She looked a bit of a mess too! She was in *winter* uniform, but with a green blouse instead of a white one.

'Don't look at me,' she said to Emma. 'Dad fetched my clothes out of the house, and *this* was his selection.' She pulled a face.

'Our Dad got mine too — so I'm sockless,' laughed Emma. 'Was your house damaged?'

'Yes, the roof's off, so we're staying out at Strubby with my Gran, until it's mended,' said Audrey.

'Bit of a squash,' joined in Tommy, 'but not much else we can do.'

'What about you?' asked Audrey. 'Your house copped it, like ours.'

'Well, we're camping out at the old school,' replied Emma. 'Spent last night in the Dane John shelter.'

They had drifted away from the boys. She turned and called out. 'Bye. See you after school.'

'Bye,' they called back.

Boys and girls seemed to be separating into groups, waiting for the whistle. It went and everyone stood still. Mr Sparke appeared with a loud hailer.

'Good morning boys and girls,' he said. 'A great deal has happened to us all, since we were last at school. Much has been lost in this terrible attack. Houses, schools and people — we will never forget the sadness that the blitz has brought.

'Before we move on to practical matters, if any of you have personal problems caused by the loss of loved ones, please know that a member of staff for each school has offered to be available for you to talk to. Sometimes, an adult who is not directly involved, can listen and help — or just listen.

'Miss Plath on the girls' staff and Mr Elliott on the boys' staff will be available. We'll make sure the daily times are posted on the notice board.'

Emma thought of Jimmy and was glad he had Uncle Charlie and *her* family to talk to. 'How awful to feel really alone at a time like this.'

Mr Sparke was still talking.

'We have one building between two schools. Your maths, and common-sense will tell you that we cannot fit you all in at once and expect you to work.

'It has been decided,' he went on, 'that this week, the boys will have the building from eight o'clock until one o'clock and the girls, from one-fifteen until five-fifteen. Next week, the girls will come in the morning and the boys in the afternoon.

'Everyone will need to co-operate. Desks, books, paper and pens will have to be shared.

'The girls have *nothing*. So boys, be chivalrous! Come to their rescue and make sure that they are equipped to work as hard as *you* are going to.

'Boys — line up. File into your classrooms.

'Girls — please remain in the playground and Miss Cannon will speak to you.'

With remarkably little noise, the boys filed into school, presumably to begin a normal day's work.

'It feels odd,' thought Emma, 'to be sitting down to

Maths and French with all this happening outside.'

'Good morning, girls,' Duch's familiar voice boomed out. 'Get into class groups. First forms here.'

She pointed to the empty space to her right. 'Now second forms.'

Soon they were all re-assembled, waiting to hear the next order.

'It is now nine-thirty. We will not be using the school building until one-fifteen.

'Do not worry. You will *not* be staying here until five-fifteen tonight. Three-thirty will be home time, as usual. The new arrangement starts tomorrow — so warn your parents. One-fifteen here — five-fifteen leave.

'Any problems, discuss with your form mistress.'

Miss Plath leaned across and whispered to her.

'Oh yes. Today, if the siren goes, we will be using our own air-raid shelter. It has not been damaged. But after that, we will use the boys'. It will be quicker.

'Form teachers, join your classes. Take registers and discuss time-tables for the rest of the morning.'

It was the strangest school morning that Emma had ever experienced. Classes sat on blankets in scattered groups all over the playground. The air was a mixture of French, German, music, Shakespeare and mental arithmetic.

No-one looked bored.

'In fact,' thought Emma, 'everyone seems to like this open-air school — with plenty of talk, no chalk, no paper, no pens — and no books.'

Chapter Eleven

POSH NEW CLOTHES FOR JIMMY

THE boys were waiting in the playground for Emma when she came out of school at half past three.

'Funny old day,' said Jimmy.

'Not a bit like ordinary school,' said Emma. 'Even this afternoon, we were getting used to *your* desks, *your* books — your everything!'

'I looked out of the window this morning,' said Bill, 'and saw you all having a good time, just sitting around on blankets.'

'We were *working!*' protested Emma. 'Not like you this afternoon. You were all either playing games, or cheering on your favourite team.'

'Bit difficult,' said Jimmy. 'There were so many rounders games going on, that we kept getting the balls muddled up.'

They were so busy discussing the day's activities that they hardly noticed the walk back to the old school. When they went in, Mum was talking to Uncle Charlie.

'Hello, you three,' she said. 'Had a good day?'

'Not sure it was good,' said Bill. 'Interesting though.'

'Have an apple,' said Mum. 'Mr Cooper brought in a big box full.'

'He's one of the local farmers,' she told Uncle Charlie. 'Try one. Good Kentish apples.'

They each took an apple and made quite a lot of noise as they scrunched their first juicy bite.

'Bill and Emma,' said Mum, 'will you go out and find Fran and Jonty. They're playing with Ginger round the back somewhere. We'd just like to have a chat with Jimmy.'

'O.K.' said Bill.

Emma looked at Jimmy. The laughter had gone from his mouth and eyes. 'He's got to talk about things that hurt,' she thought.

As she walked away with Bill, she felt terrible, wishing she could help him, but knew that the painful subject of the funeral had to be discussed.

'Will they talk about Yorkshire?' she asked Bill.

'Dunno,' he replied. 'Must wait and see.'

They found Fran and Jonty with Ginger. Bill joined in and they all began rolling down the grassy slopes.

'Don't get your uniform dirty,' Emma called to Bill. 'Mum can't wash it, you know.'

'Good clean grass,' called back Bill.

Fran and Jonty giggled and rolled after him.

Emma sat on the top of the bank, her knees hunched up, thinking. Perhaps not thinking, as much as worrying. She sensed that the next few days were going to be very difficult.

It seemed ages before Mum came to fetch them. Bill and the two little ones were still rolling. Looking at Bill's grassy shirt, Mum said, 'He'll be going to school in a striped shirt tomorrow — not the school colours either!'

She sat on the bank beside Emma. 'Will you look after Fran and Jonty on Saturday morning?' she asked.

'Course,' said Emma, not needing to ask why. She felt

relieved that this would be her contribution.

'Then Charlie's taking Jimmy to Yorkshire immediately afterwards,' continued Mum.

'On Saturday?' asked Emma, with a sense of shock. Today was Wednesday — only two more days.

'Yes,' said Mum. 'He thought it would be a good idea to get Jimmy away and not hang around afterwards.'

'What did Jimmy say?' asked Emma.

'He looked dumbstruck, at first,' replied Mum.

'*Then* what did he say?' Emma persisted.

'After a little, he agreed that it would be a good idea to get all the painful things over in one day,' said Mum.

'Jimmy's not one to sit around doing nothing and feeling sorry for himself,' said Emma. 'Do you think he minds leaving us?'

Mum slipped her arm around Emma's shoulders.

'Yes,' she assured her. 'He does — says he'll miss us.'

'Yorkshire's such a long way away,' said Emma sadly. 'We'll probably never see him again. It'll be as if the *whole* Turner family has gone —' she burst into tears.

Mum hugged her as she sobbed.

'Have a good cry with me, my pet,' she said, 'and then be brave in front of Jimmy.'

Bill stopped rolling and climbed the bank towards them. He looked anxiously at Emma.

'Everything O.K.?' he asked.

Emma dried her eyes on Mum's handkerchief.

'As right as it can be,' said Mum. 'The funeral is on Saturday morning and Emma will look after Fran and Jonty.'

'*Is* the band playing?' asked Bill.

'Yes,' said Mum. 'Jimmy *really* wanted that and Dad's said he'll get some of the chaps together for a practice on Friday night.'

'Will Jimmy play?' asked Bill doubtfully.

'Course he will,' said Emma. 'That's why he wants the band there. He'll have his cornet to hold on to and something else to think about.'

'Yes,' ageed Mum. 'I think that's the only way he feels he can cope.'

'I *do* understand,' said Bill. 'I think I'd feel the same.'

'Tell Bill about Yorkshire,' said Emma.

'Has he decided to go?' Bill asked.

'Yes,' replied Mum. 'Charlie's taking him on the train at mid-day on Saturday.'

'On *Saturday!*' Bill was astounded. 'That's so soon.'

'P'raps it's best like that,' said Mum.

'Maybe,' Bill agreed reluctantly.

Mum jumped up. 'Come on,' she said. 'Emma, brush that grass off Bill's shirt. It's time for tea.' She went to fetch Fran, Jonty and Ginger.

Vigorously, Emma brushed Bill's back.

'Not so hard,' he protested.

'If I don't brush hard, you'll have to take your shirt off and shake it,' returned Emma.

'Good idea,' said Bill and whipped his shirt off. He shook — and shook again. *Most* of the bits came off, but he looked at his white shirt in horror. Green grass stains and dirty streaks covered it.

'Wow!' he exclaimed. 'Can you wash it Mum? Will it dry before tomorrow?'

'No — I can't wash it,' she replied firmly. 'If we're lucky, Dad will have gone into the house to get some clean clothes. If not, you'll have to go to school tomorrow in *that.*'

'Or your pyjama jacket,' Emma put in with a chuckle.

'Shut up,' said Bill and shot her a cross look, 'and don't say "I told you so"!'

Emma bit her tongue and did *not* say, 'Well, I did.' She thought it though.

They wandered back into the old school for tea. Jimmy and Uncle Charlie were nowhere to be seen.

'Where are they?' Mum asked the ARP lady.

'Jimmy's uncle has taken him off to the Civic Centre to sort out some clothes for him,' she replied.

'Do they have some there, then?' asked Mum, surprised.

'Evidently,' replied the ARP lady. 'Various second-hand clothes have been given to help people like Jimmy, who lost everything when their homes were bombed.'

'How did Uncle Charlie know?' asked Mum. 'I didn't.'

'Mr King popped in and had a cup of tea with them whilst you were outside,' replied the ARP lady. 'I *think* he came in especially to tell them that.'

'He's really a very kind man,' said Mum. 'Even though a lot of children are afraid of him.'

'Only those who play truant from school,' laughed the ARP lady.

'Not only those,' thought Emma. She remembered the day, when she was quite young, sitting on their red front door-step, drawing lovely pictures with lumps of white chalk from Hollow Lane. Mr King had ridden by on his big, black bike. He stopped and walked towards her. His face looked stern and he towered above her.

'You wait 'til your Mum sees that,' he had said in a very quiet voice. 'You'd better clean it off fast.'

Emma remembered trembling and starting to cry, as she suddenly realised what she'd done.

Mum spent ages polishing the step to keep it red and shining — now she had ruined it. As Mr King got back on his bike, she pulled out her handkerchief and desperately began rubbing. Her handkerchief was not big enough, so she crept round the back into the scullery, pinched a duster before Mum could see her, and scuttled back up the alley to the front door.

With duster and spit she got rid of her lovely pictures. The step was not perfect, but it was better.

Emma remembered this and knew that it had taken her a *very* long time to like Mr King again and not be afraid of him.

As they took their baked beans, bread and mugs of tea back to their corner, Emma suddenly remembered that she had not told Mum about tomorrow. There were so many things happening — nothing was normal any more.

As they settled down, she said, 'Mum, I haven't got to go to school tomorrow until quarter past one.'

'And I've got to be there at eight o'clock,' joined in Bill.

'I was going to ask how they'd solved the space problem,' said Mum.

'Well, you going off early, Bill, is no problem,' she continued. 'What do we do with you, Emma?'

'You'll be here, won't you Mum?' asked Emma anxiously.

'I hadn't planned to be,' replied Mum. 'Fran and Jonty can go to school tomorrow, so I was going to take them and then spend the day in the house, cleaning up.'

'Well,' said Emma in a relieved voice. 'I'll help you.' Like Jimmy, she was happier when she was doing something.

'What about the roof?' asked Bill.

'Dad was hoping to get hold of a tarpaulin today,' said Mum, 'and some of his friends have promised to help him put it on, after work.'

'Good job it hasn't rained since the bombs,' said Bill, 'otherwise there would have been an even bigger mess.'

'Yes, we're lucky,' agreed Mum.

'What about gas and electricity?' asked Emma.

'Everyone's working like mad to sort it out,' said Mum, 'and we hope it will be O.K. by tomorrow.'

'What about water?' asked Bill.

'Well, we'll have to go on boiling it for quite a few weeks.' said Mum. 'At least, that's what they say.'

As they scraped their plates and rubbed their bread round to get the last drop of tomato sauce, Jimmy and Uncle Charlie came through the door with a case and some bags.

'You've obviously got some,' said Mum.

'Yes,' agreed Uncle Charlie. 'They were very helpful.'

'Never been so well dressed in my life,' said Jimmy. 'Some *very* posh blazers and trousers in this lot,' and he patted the case.

'Any spare shirts?' asked Bill hopefully.

'Bill,' said Mum reprovingly. 'Those clothes have been given to Jimmy.'

Jimmy eyed Bill's shirt. 'Made a bit of a mess of that,' he commented. 'Look. Tell you what, I've got one of your shirts on. I'll keep it and give you one out of the bag.'

Bill thought this was a very good way of getting a clean shirt. Mum looked doubtfully at Uncle Charlie.

'Great idea,' said Uncle Charlie. 'Let Bill take his pick.'

Jimmy opened the bags and cases and all of the children sat admiring the selection of clothes, whilst the grown-ups carried on talking.

Chapter Twelve

THIS HORRIBLE WAR

NEXT morning, after another night on the hard bunks in the Dane John shelter, Bill and Jimmy set off for school early. As Emma waved goodbye, she knew she was going to miss the fun of walking to school with them.

'Funny,' she thought, 'I seem to be getting on better with Bill, now that Jimmy's here. We're not arguing nearly as much. Wonder why?'

'Come on, Emma, breakfast,' called Mum and they settled down with the usual bread, margarine, red jam and mugs of tea. Emma found herself missing Mum's porridge. When she was at home, she hated it, made more with water than milk. But now, she could just imagine the brown sugar dissolving on top and improving the taste as the grey, lumpy mixture slid down.

'I'm fed up with bread and jam for breakfast,' moaned Jonty. 'Can't we have something else?'

'Be quiet,' said Mum. 'You're lucky to have that.'

'When can we go home?' wailed Fran. 'I'm getting fed up with eating on the floor.'

'It's like one long picnic,' said Mum cheerfully.

'I'll *never* like picnics again,' said Fran firmly.

'Stop moaning, you two,' interrupted Emma. 'We're the

lucky ones. Think about poor Jimmy.'

'Go on,' said Mum. 'Wash your sticky hands and get ready for school.'

'At least we don't have to wash properly,' whispered Jonty. 'Just face and hands.'

'Wait 'til I scrub you down at home,' laughed Mum. 'There'll be a lot of dirt to come off.'

Soon they were all walking down the path towards the alley, which would take them to Winfield School.

'Race you to the railway bridge,' said Emma and the two little ones rushed off. They all arrived at the bridge panting and climbed the wooden steps.

'A train's coming,' said Jonty excitedly.

'Come on, into the middle of the bridge,' said Emma. They moved across and stood watching the steaming train come towards them. Mum remained at the top of the steps. Fran and Jonty were jumping up and down in anticipation.

'Here it comes. Shut your eyes,' shouted Emma and soon they were enclosed in thick, white steam. The train rumbled beneath them and let out a loud whistle as it approached the station.

Slowly, they opened their eyes and Mum came up, laughing.

'I lost you,' she said. 'Couldn't see *any* of you. Like a thick, foggy blanket hiding you all.'

She took out a hanky and wiped the black specks from their faces.

'Let's wait for the next one,' pleaded Jonty.

'No,' said Mum firmly. 'You'll be late for school. Down the other steps and into the orchards.'

'We might find some apples on the ground,' said Emma and at once they ran off in search of the next bit of fun.

'That's one way of getting them to school,' laughed Mum. She watched as Fran picked up a big, green apple

from the ground and saw her face change as she turned it over. A bird had had a large peck out of it. Fran threw it down in disgust.

Emma looked up at the branches laden with apples, overhanging the path.

'We could easily pick a few,' she said to Mum.

'Oh no, we couldn't,' said Mum. 'Those apples belong to Mr Cooper. He was kind enough to *give* us a big bag-full yesterday.'

'O.K.,' said Emma, still eyeing the apples. 'Be different if we didn't know Mr Cooper. You can't really go scrumping* from someone you know — and like.'

* Stealing apples.

95

'You can't really go scrumping from *anyone*,' said Mum, 'even if you don't know them, or don't like them.'

'Boys do,' protested Emma.

'Not Bill, I hope,' said Mum.

'Oh no,' said Emma quickly. 'I'm sure Bill doesn't,' although she was not really too sure.

'When you're older, my girl,' went on Mum,'You can go apple picking in the school holidays. Earn yourself some pocket money and eat as many apples as you like.'

'Smashing,' said Emma. 'Better than hop-picking. You can't eat hops and your hands get black — absolutely black.'

They were walking between the hop fields now and Emma looked at the empty poles and wires. The bines were still lying in heaps on the ground. The leaves were turning brown, waiting for men to come and clean the fields up for winter.

'It *is* fun hop-picking,' said Emma, remembering the great times they had each year, sitting on their old stools, picking hops into baskets, whilst they sang and played guessing games.

'More like a holiday, than paid work,' went on Emma.

'Yes, it's only a few weeks ago that we were all there, scratching away,' said Mum sadly. 'A lot has happened since then.'

Emma knew Mum was thinking about the Turners. They all went hop-picking together — or they had done. Next year it would be different — very different.

Sadness swept over Emma again. Perhaps they should not have walked this way, but gone round the road. She loved this way. It was much more exciting than ordinary pavements and roads.

At last they came to the end of the alley and Fran and Jonty stood waiting by Lime Kiln Road. It was a bumpy road and every now and again, lorries clattered down, leaving a trail of white dust behind them.

No lorries were bumping towards them, so they crossed to the lane behind the houses. Emma could see damaged roofs peeping above the fences. A few were covered with green tarpaulin sheets.

'Will our house look like that?' asked Emma, pointing to one of them.

' 'Fraid so,' said Mum.

'But where have all these people been staying, whilst the mess is being cleaned up?' Emma asked.

'Well, remember,' replied Mum, 'some of them were evacuated at the beginning of the war — and haven't come back — so their houses are empty.'

'Yes, of course,' said Emma, 'and a lot of the Dads have been called up.'

'That's right,' said Mum. 'Others have relations in the villages and have gone there.'

'That's it,' said Emma. 'Tommy and Audrey are staying with their Gran out at Strubby.'

'Then some old people have gone up to Mount Fields,' said Mum. 'Like Mrs Farmer.'

'And Moggy Adams,' said Fran.

'Is she up there too?' Mum sounded surprised. 'I thought — I thought, she had been killed when her house was bombed.'

'No,' said Emma. 'I forgot we hadn't told you. She crawled under the counter and was saved.'

'Pity the staff at The Mount with Fanny Farmer *and* Moggy Adams,' laughed Mum.

'They're in the same ward,' added Emma.

'My goodness,' said Mum. 'Poor nurses. I think I ought to go and visit them.'

'Do you have to?' asked Emma.

'Well, neither of them have relations,' said Mum. 'Perhaps this evening.'

'If the boys look after Fran and Jonty,' said Emma, 'I'll come with you.' She did not want to, but knew it would be hard for Mum.

'That's nice of you,' said Mum. 'Let's see.'

By now, they had reached the school gates. Fran and Jonty were waiting.

'Can we go in?' they asked.

'I'll come too,' said Mum, 'just to make sure everything's all right.'

Emma waited whilst Mum took the two little ones into the playground and spoke to the teacher on duty. There did not seem to be many children there. 'Where are they all?' was the question in Emma's mind.

'I hope — I hope,' she thought, 'they're all still alive — somewhere.' She was glad she was not a teacher calling the register at Winfield School today. It had been bad enough at her school yesterday — the empty places — not knowing where those girls were. The little ones could be even more upset, not knowing and not really understanding.

'War is horrible,' thought Emma. '*Quite* horrible.'

'Why doesn't someone stop it?' she muttered aloud.

'Why doesn't someone stop what?' asked a familiar voice beside her. She turned round, startled. It was Old Mike.

'What are you doing here?' she asked in surprise.

'Well, the little Shepherd kids were in the shelter with me last night,' said Mike. 'Their Dad has been shot down and their Mum is too upset to do anything just now, so I'm helping their Granny look after them.'

'Good Old Mike,' thought Emma. 'Helping out again.'

'That's sad for Mrs Shepherd,' she said aloud and her voice trailed off. 'Very sad.'

What else could she say? This horrible, horrible war.

'I was really wondering, why someone doesn't stop the war,' she confessed to Old Mike.

'I know how you feel,' he said, 'but Churchill is trying. I'm glad we've got him in charge.'

'Yes,' said Emma. 'When I hear him talk on the wireless, I really can *believe* him.'

'Well, keep believing, Em,' said Old Mike. 'How's young Jimmy?'

'He's going to Yorkshire on Saturday,' said Emma, 'to live with his Grandma.'

'That's probably the best thing he can do,' said Mike.

'We'll miss him,' said Emma.

'He'll come back, one day,' said Mike. 'I know he'll come back — if only to see a lovely young lass like you.'

'I'm not lovely,' said Emma and pulled an embarrassed face. 'All long and skinny.'

'You're lovelier than you think, madam,' said Mike. 'One day all the boys will be after you — including Jimmy Turner.'

Emma blushed. She could not really believe this but it was a very nice thought.

Mum came back as the whistle blew. The little ones stood still — perfectly still. The whistle blew again and they filed silently into school.

'Everything O.K., Mrs Bart?' asked Mike.

'Fine,' said Mum. 'We're going back home to do some cleaning. How about you?'

'I came to bring the Shepherd children,' replied Mike. 'You heard about their Dad?'

'Yes,' said Mum. 'I do hope he's O.K. A prisoner-of-war, or something.'

'Just posted missing at the moment,' said Mike. 'That's hard. Very hard — not knowing what's happened.'

'I know. I'm very sorry,' said Mum. 'We'd better be off to start that cleaning. Emma's got to go to school this afternoon, so we're not going to have much time.'

'Bye, Mike,' said Emma. 'See you in the shelter, or somewhere.'

They walked off towards the house and Emma began to wonder exactly what they *would* find inside.

Chapter Thirteen

SOOT!

As they rounded the corner, they saw the house with its green cover dangling over the damaged roof. Not just *their* house, but almost every house in the row was covered. Some chimney stacks were damaged and most of the chimney pots were on the pavements, smashed into a number of pieces.

'Hi there, Bart,' called Mrs Petts, as she emerged from her front door with a shovel and broom. 'Just trying to get rid of some of the mess.'

'Have you finished indoors?' asked Mum.

'Haven't even started,' replied Mrs Petts, pulling a face. 'I'm just gathering my strength,' she laughed.

'Where are you staying?' asked Mum.

'Over at Keetham with my mother-in-law,' she said. 'I've left the kids there, whilst I try to get the house cleaned up. What about you?'

'We're round at the old school during the day,' replied Mum 'and in the Dane John shelter at night.'

'Bit uncomfortable day *and* night,' said Mrs Petts, looking concerned.

'Yes — but at least we're all alive and well,' said Mum.

'You're right,' agreed Mrs Petts. 'It's wrong to moan about little things.'

'Think we'd better go and get started,' said Mum. 'Bye.'

'Bye,' returned Mrs Petts and they left her shovelling up the bits of chimney pots and broken glass.

They reached the house and walked down the alley. Mum unlocked the back door and they went in. The kitchen floor was a bit muddy and the table, dusty, but apart from that, not too bad. It was very different in the living room. Everything was covered in black soot.

Mum ran her finger across the table, leaving a clear line.

'How do we get rid of this lot?' asked Emma. She looked down at her school uniform doubtfully.

'Look,' said Mum. 'I'm going upstairs to get us both some old clothes. We'll go into the shelter to change and leave these clothes on the bunks.'

'Never thought of that black hole being clean, until now,' laughed Emma.

'It's all comparison,' said Mum. 'Don't touch *anything* — just go back outside.'

Emma retreated to the shelter and sat gloomily on the bunk. She wanted to help. She had *expected* it to be dirty and messy, but not that horrid, black soot.

'To think that that's normally up the chimney,' she mused.

'Fancy being a chimney sweep and spending your life brushing soot down. No wonder Mr Petts never looks clean. How *could* he? Every morning, every afternoon, pushing his brushes up chimneys and getting down sackfuls of soot.'

She shuddered at the thought.

'Here — put these on.' Mum reappeared at the top of the shelter steps and handed Emma some clothes that she had not seen for years.

'These have got holes in,' she said.

'I know,' said Mum. 'We'll throw them away after.'

Back in the house, Emma wondered where they would start.

'Brush and dust pan first,' said Mum and handed Emma her tools. 'Start at the top and work down. I'll go on the steps and brush the picture rail, you come behind and brush the skirting*.'

'Pity there isn't something that will just suck it all up.' groaned Emma.

'Perhaps there will be, one day,' said Mum, hopefully.

'Perhaps we won't even have soot,' said Emma, even more hopefully.

'You can't have fires without soot and you can't keep warm without fires,' observed Mum.

* Narrow board along bottom of room wall.

'Well,' said Emma. 'We have radiators at school.'

'Yes,' agreed Mum, 'but there's a big fire in the boiler house heating the water.'

As they talked, they gently brushed. Piles of soot fell into the dustpans — but lots floated gently into the air.

'It'll land somewhere else,' thought Emma.

Mum suddenly jumped down from the steps.

'Just remembered,' she said. 'You're going to school this afternoon and your hair will be black. We can't wash it.'

She ran upstairs and came down with two scarves.

'Come on,' she said, 'let's put these on like girls in the munitions* factories.'

Soon, they both had tight little caps on their heads.

'Glad I can't see myself in the mirror,' laughed Emma.

They brushed, they dusted, they used damp cloths, until everything they were using was black.

'A bit like hop-picking,' said Emma, 'except that soot smells even worse than hops.'

'I *like* the smell of hops,' protested Mum. She looked at her watch.

'We must go back to the old school and get you cleaned up ready for school,' she said.

'Wish I could stay,' said Emma. 'I think I'd be a bit more use here.'

'*You* are going to school, my girl,' said Mum firmly.

'Look,' said Emma. 'I'll go, but if you'd like to stay on here, I can easily run back on my own.'

'Suppose the siren goes?' Mum was dubious.

'I'll dash for the shelter,' replied Emma. 'Since we've had these barrage balloons, it's all been much quieter.'

Reluctantly, Mum agreed. She pushed the school clothes into a bag.

* War weapons.

104

'Wash in warm water before you touch these,' she said. 'I've put some soap and a towel at the bottom.'

She waved goodbye to Emma and laughed, 'If you meet anyone you know, they won't recognise you.'

Emma laughed too as she ran off down the middle of the road. That, at least, was clear of rubble. Conscious of what Mum had said about how awful she looked, she stopped at the corner.

Which way should she go?

If she went through the orchards, she was less likely to meet anyone she knew — *but*, if the siren did go, there were no shelters.

If she went the road way, she knew of a number of shelters. She could easily run into the Norman Castle, the church basement, or the Dane John shelter.

Which should it be? The orchards, she decided, and just hoped that the enemy planes would stay away for about fifteen minutes.

Chapter Fourteen

ALONE – AND SCARED

SHE climbed Taggs Hill and turned towards Lime Kiln Road. She ran across the bumpy road and into the pathway by Mr Cooper's farm. Through the hop-fields she ran, not stopping to look, or think. She had just reached the orchards when a terrible bellow burst forth.

Tug-Boat Annie!

Her heart pounded. 'But the siren hasn't gone,' she inwardly protested. 'There *can't* be planes overhead — the balloons will keep them away.'

She looked up to the clear blue sky. There were no barrage balloons to be seen — and she remembered that they had been taken down yesterday morning. At the same time, she heard the drone of planes.

'What can I do?' she panicked. 'There are *no* shelters.'

She stood shaking by the gate leading into the orchard. 'Only one thing,' she decided and quickly climbed over the gate. She ran under the apple trees and she fell flat on the ground. There was a terrible whine.

A plane zoomed out of the sky — a massive explosion followed. The ground beneath her shook — and she shook.

'Please let it stop,' she pleaded.

Now gun-fire joined the noise of the planes and bangs — and the siren went!

'A bit late,' thought Emma.

The barrage went on and on. She buried her head in her arms to shut out the noise.

'Don't let anyone be killed, *please* don't let anyone be killed,' she kept saying.

The planes droned off into the distance. The explosions stopped and Emma sat up, still shaking.

'Where have those bombs fallen?' she worried to her herself.

Everyone was separated this morning. Bill and Jimmy, Fran and Jonty, at different schools, Mum at home — and Dad? Where was Dad? As these thoughts chased through her mind, Tug-Boat Annie bellowed forth its single note. The planes were no longer overhead. She thought she had better lie still until the siren sounded its 'All Clear'.

Where should she go? Home to Mum? She was almost too frightened to do that. Suppose one of those bombs had fallen on their house. She could not, she *couldn't*, discover that alone.

'Stop thinking like that,' Emma told herself firmly. 'Get back to the old school. That's where Mum expects you to be.'

The 'All Clear' warbled forth. She grabbed the bag of school clothes and climbed the orchard gate, back onto the path. She felt some wet patches on her clothes and realised, for the first time, that she must have been lying on some squashed apples. She had been too frightened to feel uncomfortable.

'Thank goodness I hadn't changed into my school uniform,' she thought. 'I must look even messier now — soot and squashed apples don't make a very good combination!'

She resolved that as soon as she got to the old school, she would try to get to the cloakroom, before she saw anyone. Thankfully she reached the railway bridge and was glad no trains were coming. This was no time to have fun in the steam. She looked towards the station.

To her horror, she saw piles of rubble and clouds of smoke rising from where the station had been. She began to tremble again. The station had been hit. Was there a train standing there? She hoped not. That would mean even more people had been hurt, or killed.

For the first time, the thought struck her that the old school might have been damaged.

'The explosion at the station would have blown out the windows,' she thought. 'Be a bit draughty.'

She ran on down the alley, not meeting anyone and emerged onto the pavement opposite the Dane John Mound*. She looked towards the old school. She gasped in horror.

* Burial mound — probably Roman.

The old school had received a direct hit. Everything had collapsed and on top of the mini-mound was a pile of broken bricks, huge chimney stacks, doors, windows, bricks and flints. The main door and the window frame of Miss Hogben's room remained standing in eerie isolation.

Still Emma could not move. The shock was immense. Suddenly, she felt a tap on her shoulder that made her jump. She turned round quickly. It was Dad! He looked at her with mixed amazement and joy.

'I didn't recognise you at first,' he said. 'Thank God you're safe.' He folded her in his arms.

'Where's Mum? Where's Mum?' he asked, his voice full of anxiety.

'She's at home, still cleaning,' said Emma. She was afraid to ask about their house. If it could happen to the old school and the station, it could happen anywhere.

Dad saw her face and said gently, 'I don't know about our house. I just heard about the old school and was terrified that you and Mum were there.'

'What shall we do?' Emma asked tearfully. 'Shall we go together and find out?'

Dad nodded. 'Yes, we'll go together,' he said. 'You certainly can't stay here. Let me just go and speak to the ARP men. I'll let them know that none of you were inside when the bomb fell.'

He walked up the slope to where men were already beginning to work on the ruined building. Emma hoped that the ARP ladies had not been trapped inside. They had been so kind and good.

Dad walked back down to her with a very unhappy look on his face. 'They think there were about twenty people inside, having dinner,' he said.

'That's terrible,' said Emma and began shaking again.

'I've said I'll take you home to see if Mum's all right,' said

Dad, 'and then come back to help.'

They hurried silently back along the orchard paths, until they finally reached the top of Tagg's Hill. Emma felt afraid to go down to the corner and look.

'Dad,' she said quietly, 'will you go on to the corner and tell me that everything's O.K.?'

Dad squeezed her hand and ran to the bottom of the hill. Emma knew he was scared too. He reached the corner. Looked to the left. Turned round and put up his thumbs.

'Come on,' he called. 'The house is still there.' He sounded so relieved. Emma ran down to him and they hurried along to No. 39.

As they reached the alley, Mum appeared, still wearing her turban and covered in soot. She looked as if she had been crying. The tears had left streaks through the soot on her face. She rushed up to them.

'Emma, Emma,' she cried. 'Thank God you're safe. Mr King has just told me about the old school and I was terrified that you might have got there before the bomb fell.'

She hugged Emma. 'Where were you?' she asked.

'Under the trees in the orchard,' said Emma. 'I was *so* frightened.'

'So was I,' admitted Mum, 'in the shelter on my own and not knowing where you and Dad were. Then, worrying about the others at school.'

'Let's go into the house for a minute and discuss what we're going to do,' said Dad. 'There's no old school to go to.' He looked thoughtful.

They went into the living room. 'That looks cleaner,' said Dad, admiringly.

'But it's not clean enough,' replied Mum, 'and I haven't done *anything* else.' They both looked worried.

'We can't move back until we've got the front room cleaned and furniture shifted around,' she went on.

'Yes,' agreed Dad. 'We've got to hump the armchairs and everything upstairs and bring beds down. The piano will have to stay.'

'I don't see how we can manage all that before Sunday, at the earliest,' said Mum, 'however much we try.'

'You could go up Hollow Lane to sleep,' suggested Dad, 'but Dot hasn't got room for Jimmy as well.'

'We can't leave him out,' said Mum. 'He needs us now, more than ever. After Saturday, that's different. But until then, we *must* stay with him.'

Emma hesitated joining in the discussion, seeing their anxious faces, but she *did* have a good idea.

'Can't we work hard on this room and the kitchen,' she said, 'and decide that we're all going to sleep in the shelter, until we get the beds down?'

'Tell you what,' Dad said. 'The boys and I will sleep on the floor in here, unless the siren goes. The rest of you can use the bunks in the shelter. How's that?'

Both Mum and Emma looked relieved. At least they would be living at home, how ever awful it was.

'Now we've sorted that out,' said Dad, 'I'll go back to the old school and help them. When Bill and Jimmy come, I'll send them up here.'

'You'd better be quick,' said Mum, 'or they'll be there first — and that will be quite a shock.'

'Tell them to come the road way,' said Emma. 'At least they can dash into a shelter if anything happens.'

'Right, I'm off then,' said Dad. 'See you later.' He kissed them both and hurried out.

Chapter Fifteen

BOMBS BRING MORE CHANGES

EMMA and Mum stood silently for a moment, trying to adjust to yet another change in their living arrangements.

'War doesn't half upset things,' said Emma. 'You never know what's going to happen next.'

'I know,' said Mum. 'But we are *still* lucky — we're all together.'

'I wonder who the twenty people were in the old school,' Emma said quietly, her anxiety showing in her voice. She had been so concerned, until then, with their small problems, that she had almost forgotten the really big problems that other people had.

Mum gave her a hug. 'Come on, let's do some work,' she said, and handed Emma some clean pieces of old sheet. 'We'll have to use these. I've run out of dusters.'

They scrubbed, brushed, dusted and polished until, gradually, the room began to look more normal. Mum straightened herself up.

'I could do with a cup of tea,' she said.

'I could do with a drink — and I'm jolly hungry,' said Emma. 'I'd forgotten about food until now.'

'Wow!' said Mum. 'So had I. Really don't know what we've got in the house and whether it's worth eating.'

She went into the kitchen and looked into the larder*.

'Tell you what,' she said. 'I'll make a list and when the boys come, they could go round to the shop for me.'

'They'll be cleaner than we are,' laughed Emma.

'What about tea?' asked Mum.

'Is there any gas?' asked Emma.

'We'll soon find out,' said Mum and turned on the tap. She held out a lighted match — and the gas flames shot up.

'Thank goodness,' she said. 'At least I can cook.' She filled the kettle and put it on to boil.

'We haven't any fresh milk,' she said. 'It'll have to be condensed. When the boys go round to Wilton's, they can go down to Parkers. Mrs P. always has about half a churn left after the round's finished.'

'They must remember to take a jug then,' said Emma.

'Now, what can we eat with this tea,' said Mum.

'I know,' said Emma, 'my iron# rations. They've been in my gas mask box for ages, so it'll be a good thing to eat them.'

She dashed into the air-raid shelter and grabbed her gas mask box.

'We forgot to take these with us when we went to the old school,' she said, as she came back into the house. 'Everyone's been so busy after the bombing, that they've forgotten to check up on them — even at school.'

She lifted her gas mask out of the box and underneath, was a small, sealed tin. She pulled off the sticking plaster and peeped inside.

'Two small bars of chocolate and some peppermints,' she said. 'I'd almost forgotten.'

They munched the chocolate, which was slightly faded with age and Mum poured tea into two mugs. She opened a

* Cupboard for storing food.   # Emergency rations.

tin of condensed milk, dipped a teaspoon into the white, sticky substance and lifted it straight into Emma's cup.

Emma gently stirred and the milk dissolved into the hot liquid. She was not really keen on condensed milk — it was too sweet. But, there was no choice. She swallowed the tea and grabbed a peppermint.

'That's a better taste,' she thought as she sucked the sweet.

They were just finishing, when the door opened and the boys came in. They both looked very subdued.

'Hello,' said Mum. 'Good to see you. Want some tea?'

'Please,' they both said.

'Anything to eat?' asked Bill.

'Well, no,' said Mum. 'I want you to go to the shop.'

'You've been eating some chocolate,' he protested.

'My iron rations,' said Emma.

'Good idea,' said Bill. 'Where's my gas-mask?'

'In the Anderson*,' said Emma, and he ran out of the back door into the shelter.

'I'm not sure where mine is,' said Jimmy, looking doubtful.

'Never mind,' said Bill, as he returned. 'Share mine.'

As they munched and drank, Mum was making a shopping list.

'Did you see the old school?' asked Emma.

'Awful,' said Bill. 'I don't think I want to talk about what we saw.'

He and Jimmy exchanged troubled glances. They were both upset. Seeing how they looked, Emma was afraid to ask any more questions. She was sure that they were unhappy about people — not just the building.

Mum appeared with a shopping list, a purse, two large bags and ration books.

'I think there are enough coupons for everything,' she said.

'Hope so,' said Bill. 'Right. We'll go.'

'What about the jug?' asked Emma.

'Oh yes,' said Mum. 'Take a jug and get a pint of milk from Mrs Parker.'

'Good,' said Jimmy. 'I like watching her measure it out.'

'I'm not carrying it back,' said Bill. 'I'll spill it. I'll carry the bags — and you take the jug.' The boys went off.

'Front room next,' said Mum. She gathered the dustpan, brushes and cloths up and walked through the living room into the hall. As they opened the front room door, Emma could see that this room was as bad as the living room had been. Soot, soot, soot.

They went to work. Mum at the top and Emma at the bottom.

* Type of air-raid shelter.

'Pity poor Tom,' said Emma.

'Tom who?' asked Mum.

'Tom in The Water Babies,' replied Emma. 'He had to climb down chimneys, brushing the soot as he came. How perfectly awful!'

'It wasn't just Tom in the story,' said Mum, 'but lots and lots of other young boys, who had to work like that.'

'Girls seemed to escape,' said Emma.

Mum glanced at the clock. 'I think you'd better start cleaning yourself up, if you're going with the boys to meet Fran and Jonty from school,' she said.

Emma *wanted* to go. She hated the smell, taste and feel of soot for one thing. But there was another reason. Jimmy was going to Yorkshire very soon and she wanted to spend some more time with him.

Her first thought was to say, 'O.K. I'll get ready.' But she did not. She heard herself saying, 'Let the boys go. I'll stay and help you.'

The look on Mum's face was her reward. They worked on until they heard the back door open and the boys coming in.

'Where shall we put it?' called Bill.

'Leave it there,' Mum called back. 'Any problems?'

'Well, Wilton's were out of dried eggs*,' said Bill as he came into the front room.

'That's a nuisance,' said Mum.

'But, we've done better than that,' said Jimmy over Bill's shoulder. 'We were chatting to Mrs Parker as she measured out the milk and she suddenly asked us if we wanted a dozen eggs!'

'But you didn't have enough money for fresh eggs,' said Mum, looking worried.

*Fresh eggs made into a yellow powder.

116

'We didn't *need* any money,' said Bill. 'She *gave* us the eggs as a present.'

'How kind,' said Mum.

'Some of her regular customers have gone off to the villages,' said Jimmy, 'so she had some left over.'

'What about coupons?' asked Mum.

'She didn't want any,' said Bill. 'Said something about these being from garden chickens — not farm chickens. Don't quite understand the difference.'

'Let's enjoy them,' said Mum. 'I think we could do with a treat.'

'That's exactly what Mrs Parker said,' commented Jimmy.

'Now will you please go and fetch Fran and Jonty from school,' said Mum.

'Aren't you coming, Em?' Jimmy asked, looking disappointed.

Under the soot, Emma felt herself blushing. 'Well,' she said, 'I was going to carry on helping Mum.'

Bill looked at them both. 'Tell you what,' he said. 'I'll put some old clothes on. You quickly clean yourself up, Em and go with Jimmy.'

Mum was not quite sure what to make of his generous offer — but she gave a warm smile and edged Emma out of the front room.

'There's a drop of hot water in the kettle,' she said, 'but get as much off as you can with cold first.'

Emma never thought she could clean herself up as quickly. Clean hands, legs, face and clothes. Mum pulled the scarf off her head and brushed her hair.

'Almost back to normal,' laughed Emma. She pulled down the sleeves of her blouse to hide the black lines and joined Jimmy outside.

'Ready,' she said. Mum and Bill watched them walk off together.

'Funny that,' said Bill. 'Never thought Jimmy Turner would fancy my sister.'

'What do you mean?' asked Mum. 'Fancy your sister?'

'Well, as a girl-friend,' replied Bill. 'She seemed too young for him, but he really *does* like her.'

'How do you know?' asked Mum.

'I just know,' replied Bill. 'Pity he's going away. We may never see him again.'

Emma felt a little awkward, as she walked out of the alley and along the road towards the school. She was thrilled that Jimmy wanted her to go with him, but strangely shy. He seemed to be tongue-tied too.

'Race you to Pett's corner,' he said and ran off. She flew after him, determined that he would not beat her by much. He did not. Breathless and laughing they turned the corner.

Before their shyness could settle on them again, Emma asked, 'Have you seen your uncle today?'

'Yes,' said Jimmy. 'He came across as we left the playground and walked up to the old school with us. He'd heard it had been bombed and wasn't sure what we'd find when we got there,'

'Nice of him,' said Emma.

Jimmy stopped and looked at her.

'You know, I was quaking inside as we walked,' he said. 'I was terrified that you and your mother were in the building.'

'Would — would it have mattered to you?' asked Emma with some hesitation.

'It would have mattered very much,' he said. Emma felt herself blushing.

'You know Em,' he went on. 'I'm glad to be going to

Yorkshire to see my Gran and Uncle Charlie's family, but I shall *really* miss the Barts.'

'Yorkshire seems so far away,' said Emma sadly.

'It doesn't just seem — it *is!*' said Jimmy with feeling.

They walked on, conscious that mothers were gathering in groups and chatting, as they hurried to meet their children from school.

'Will you write to me, Em?' asked Jimmy, shyly.

'Course I will,' replied Emma, 'if you'd like me to.' Inside she began to feel happy again — and determined that she would write very interesting letters.

'Will you write the first letter?' she asked, cautiously.

He laughed. 'O.K. That's fair,' he said. 'You can read out to the others the bits you want them to hear.'

They had now reached the school gate and stood waiting for the children to come out.

'What a nice surprise, seeing you two,' said a familiar voice — and there was Old Mike.

'What are you doing here?' asked Jimmy.

'I've come to meet the Shepherd children,' Mike replied.

'Oh yes,' said Jimmy. 'I heard that their Dad is missing. That's terrible — not to know, probably 'til the end of the war whether someone is alive, or dead. At least I *know* what's happened to my family . . .' His voice trailed off.

'You'll be glad when Saturday is over,' Mike said to him in a quiet voice, 'and you are on that train to Yorkshire.'

'Yes,' agreed Jimmy. 'I'll be glad when Saturday morning's over.' He still found it hard to say the word 'funeral'. 'When I go to Yorkshire,' he continued, 'I'll miss my friends down here.'

'Well, keep in touch,' said Mike. 'We want to know how you're doing.'

'Well,' and now it was Jimmy's turn to blush, 'Emma and

119

I have promised to write to each other, so she can pass on the news.'

Old Mike gave an impish grin and looked at Emma's pink cheeks. All he said was, 'That's great. P'raps you'll be back one day.'

The little ones rushed out. Jimmy and Emma had no more time to talk on the walk back home. Fran and Jonty chattered non-stop with all the news of the day.

Chapter Sixteen

TROUBLE FOR AUNT BERTHA

'I'M *hungry,*' wailed Jonty, as they went in through the back door.

'Thought you would be,' laughed Mum, as she kissed him. 'Have a sandwich.'

'Is it red jam?' asked Fran.

'No — not red jam,' replied Mum. 'Home-made lemon curd.'

'Smashin',' said Jonty.

'Where's Bill?' asked Jimmy.

'Still working in the front room,' said Mum.

'We'll go and help him,' said Emma.

'Yes, I'd like to, Mrs Barton,' Jimmy assured her, as she looked at him dubiously.

'O.K. You two go and help Bill,' Mum said. 'Fran and Jonty can help me make a shepherd's pie for supper.'

'Goody,' said Jonty. 'I love Mum's shepherd's pie.'

'Make a change from sausages,' laughed Emma. Then her face saddened. 'Hope those ARP ladies are O.K.'

'Come on, Em,' said Jimmy. 'Back into your dirty clothes.'

'What about you?' returned Emma. 'You can't help togged up in your school uniform.'

'Wait you two,' said Mum. 'I've put some old clothes in the shelter. Jimmy, go and take your pick. Emma, your dirty ones are still here in the kitchen.' Jimmy dashed out to the Anderson.

Quickly, Emma changed back into her horrid, sooty clothes.

Mum picked up her clean clothes.

'What's all that black stuff on you Emma?' asked Jonty.

'Soot. Nasty, horrid soot,' said Fran, 'from the chimney.'

'At least we won't have to have Mr Petts to sweep the chimneys this year,' said Mum. 'The bombs have cleaned them.'

Emma went off to find Bill. He gave her a cheeky grin.

'Well, how did you get on?' he teased.

'Fine,' said Emma, feeling her cheeks go pink. She was glad when the door opened and Jimmy came in. Bill would not ask any more questions now.

'Right, Guvner,' said Jimmy. 'What do you want us to do?'

Once again, the scrubbing, brushing, dusting and polishing went on, so did the chatting, teasing and laughing. None of them wanted to work in silence. Their thoughts would not have been happy ones.

They had just about finished, when there was a loud banging at the front door.

'Who on earth's that?' said Bill.

'Sounds official,' said Jimmy, quietly.

'Hope nothing else dreadful has happened,' thought Emma.

They stood listening as Mum opened the door.

'Mrs Barton,' said the voice of Police Sergeant Goldfinch. 'May I come in for a few minutes?'

'Oh dear,' thought Emma. 'It *must* be bad news.'

'Please do,' said Mum. 'If it's bad news, can we stand here and talk, because of the children.'

'Well,' he went on, 'it's not too bad — just difficult.'

'Difficult?' Mum questioned in a puzzled voice.

'During the raid this morning,' he said, 'an enemy plane was shot down over the town. It broke into pieces, but the pilot bailed out with his parachute.

'Unfortunately for him, he did not land on the ground, but on the roof of a house. He was killed and the parachute is draped all over a cottage in Chanters Lane.'

'Oh,' Mum exclaimed. 'Aunt Bertha's cottage.'

'Right,' agreed Police Sergeant Goldfinch, 'Bertha Wills' cottage.'

'Is *she* all right?' asked Mum anxiously.

'Yes,' he laughed. 'She's a tough old lady! I knocked on the door, but I really thought that everyone in that row had left the city.'

'They all have, except her,' said Mum.

'I was surprised when I heard her hobbling along the passage and saw her opening the door,' the police sergeant grinned. 'Do you know the first thing she said?'

'Go on,' said Mum. 'I can guess.'

'Come in — let's have a cup of tea!' he said, in amazement. 'No tears, no panic — just a perfectly normal invitation.'

'Did you get your tea?' asked Mum.

'Well, no,' he said. 'I had to persuade her that the airman's damaged plane had buried itself on a gas main and if she lit a match, we'd both be blown up.'

'Where is she now?' Mum asked anxiously.

'Still there,' he said. 'That's the problem. She won't leave.'

'I know — she's stubborn,' said Mum.

'She *would* have come to live here with you,' said Police Sergeant Goldfinch slowly.

'Here?' burst out Mum. Emma rarely heard Mum be so explosive. 'We can't *possibly* have her here. It's bad enough trying to fit ourselves in, with no upstairs.'

'This is what I tried to tell her,' said the police sergeant, 'but she wouldn't listen.'

'I'm sure she wouldn't,' said Mum, knowing what Aunt Bertha was like when she had made up her mind. 'But where *can* she go?' Mum was obviously very worried.

'Well, Mount Fields seems the only place,' said Police Sergeant Goldfinch.

'I'm sure she won't go there,' declared Mum, 'especially if she knows that Mrs Farmer and Moggy Adams are there too.'

'I mentioned that,' said the police sergeant apologetically. 'Thought it would help.'

'No, that would only make matters worse,' Mum said. 'I just don't know what we can do.'

'The problem is,' went on the police sergeant, 'not so much the damage to the house, but the leaking gas and water mains. We *must* get her out quickly.'

'There's nothing for it,' said Mum. 'She *must* go to Mount Fields.'

'Will you come and tell her?' asked Police Sergeant Goldfinch.

'Oh dear,' said Mum. 'It's one thing on top of another.'

'She sounds as if she's had enough problems for one day,' thought Emma, as she stood at the living room door, listening.

Emma looked at the boys and said, 'Will you help?'

They nodded and she opened the door into the hall.

'Mum, we couldn't help hearing,' she said. 'I'll come with you to persuade Aunt Bertha and the boys will stay here with Fran and Jonty.'

'Goody,' shouted Jonty, as his head popped round the living room door.

'We'd like that,' said Fran.

'What about supper?' asked Mum, hesitating.

'Even *we* can dish up shepherd's pie,' said Jimmy.

'Promise we'll save you some,' said Bill.

'Right then,' said Police Sergeant Goldfinch. 'Seems as if your youngsters have solved this half of the problem.'

'It's the next half that will be more difficult,' said Mum. She was smiling again. 'Thanks all of you — you're a splendid lot of kids.'

She looked worried again. 'I'm not sure how long all of this will take and Fran and Jonty will need to go to bed in the shelter,' she said.

125

'Don't worry, Mum,' said Bill. 'We'll sort it out.'

Police Sergeant Goldfinch entered the discussion again.

'If you can persuade her,' he said, 'I'll lay on transport to get her up to Mount Fields. It may have to be a jeep — or something.'

Emma started giggling. 'Aunt Bertha in a jeep,' she said.

'An adventure like that might actually persuade her to go,' laughed Mum. 'I don't think she's even been in a car, let alone a jeep!'

Mum and Emma bustled around to clean themselves up, whilst Police Sergeant Goldfinch talked to the others. Lovely smells of cooking wafted out of the oven and Emma began to feel quite hungry.

'Hope they *do* keep us some supper,' she said. 'I'm starving.'

Mum grabbed some apples from the larder.

'Come on,' she said. 'We'll nibble these as we walk through.'

'What time's Dad coming home?' asked Bill, as they returned to the living room.

'I'm not sure,' said Mum.

'He's helping at the old school, isn't he?' asked the police sergeant. Mum nodded.

'It's pretty difficult there,' he went on. 'Might take all night.'

Mum looked worried again, but said quietly, *'Somebody's* got to do the rescue work.'

She turned to Bill. 'Fran and Jonty can listen to "Children's Hour" now,' she said. 'It's five o'clock. Then perhaps you can play a few games with them after supper.'

'Either that,' said Bill, 'or we can get out the instruments and we can play and they can sing. Need to get my lip in for band practice tomorrow night.'

Jimmy looked doubtful.

'I haven't got my cornet here,' he said. 'Only my mouthpiece.'

'That's O.K.,' said Bill. 'You can borrow Dad's.'

'There'll be no Fanny Farmer knocking the wall and telling you to "shut up",' laughed Mum.

She turned to Fran and Jonty.

'Looks as if you're going to have a lovely time,' she said. 'Be good.' She gave them both a big kiss.

Emma looked at Jimmy. He was watching Mum with the little ones. A lost look came over his face.

'He is so unhappy underneath,' she thought, 'but he's trying so hard to be brave.'

He turned and caught her eyes on him. 'Bye,' he said. 'It sounds as if we'll have a better time than you will.'

Chapter Seventeen

AUNT BERTHA IN A JEEP

POLICE Sergeant Goldfinch pushed his bike, whilst Emma and Mum walked beside him through the streets of the ruined city. Finally, they arrived at Chanters Lane.

A big **ROAD CLOSED** notice greeted them. Barriers were across the street and men were working with pickaxes, shovels and wagons to clear parts of an aeroplane strewn across the road and buried in deep craters.

'Can we get through to the other end?' asked Police Sergeant Goldfinch.

'Good job he's with us,' Mum whispered to Emma.

'Sorry sergeant, not this way,' said one of the men. 'You'll have to go round past the old hospital.'

'Strict orders not to let anyone in,' said the foreman, who had come up to the group. 'Not sure you'll be allowed in the other end. Escaping gas, you see.'

'I know,' said Police Sergeant Goldfinch, 'but there's an old lady in one of the cottages — and we've *got* to get her out.'

'She's gone,' said the foreman.

'What do you mean — gone?' asked Mum, startled.

The other man laughed. 'We all stopped work to watch.

A jeep drove in the far end of the lane,' said the foreman, 'and a couple of young soldiers got out. They went into the cottage with the parachute on the roof.'

'That's the cottage,' said Mum anxiously.

'They came out a few minutes later,' went on the foreman. 'One of them had his arm round an old lady and the other was carrying her bags.'

Mum looked astounded — so did Police Sergeant Goldfinch.

'Then what?' she asked.

'They lifted her up into the jeep,' replied the foreman, 'and as they drove off, she started waving and smiling at us — just like the Queen.'

All of the men were laughing now.

'She really fancied herself,' said one of them.

'Just like Aunt Bertha,' said Mum, as she joined in the laughter. 'She'd enjoy that.'

Then she stopped laughing and said, 'They'll have more difficulty in getting her out when she gets to Mount Fields.'

'Sure they will,' said the police sergeant. 'We'd better get up there fast.'

So, with thanks to the men, they hurried off. Emma was beginning to feel tired — all the rushing around, after the frightening events of the day.

A motor-bike and side car pulled up beside them. It was Mr Cooper, the farmer.

'Can I help?' he asked.

'We're going up to Mount Fields,' said Mum and Police Sergeant Goldfinch filled him in with the story.

'Look — jump in the side-car, Mrs Bart and young Emma,' said Mr Cooper. 'The police sergeant can bike up behind us.'

Mum and Emma squeezed in the side car. 'This is fun,'

said Emma. 'Wait 'til the boys hear about it. I've never been in one of these before.'

'Nor me,' said Mum. 'Bikes, buses and trains are the only things I've had rides on.'

Police Sergeant Goldfinch and Mr Cooper had gone on talking. They turned to Mum.

'Mr Cooper has promised to help you persuade Mrs Wills,' said the sergeant, 'whilst I go and see what else needs doing.'

Mum's face lit up.

'Of course — you used to be Uncle Frank's boss,' she suddenly remembered.

'Yes, and that cottage with the parachute on is one of ours for retired workers,' Mr Cooper reminded her. 'So perhaps I *might* have some influence.'

'I'm sure your voice will be stronger than ours,' said Mum, sounding relieved. 'Then you might be able to persuade her better than we can.'

'I've also got some ideas about where she can live, whilst the repairs are being carried out,' said Mr Cooper. 'As long as she stays in Mount Fields for *one* night.'

'That really will influence her,' said Mum with conviction.

'I think so,' said Mr Cooper. 'Good girl tonight — reward tomorrow.'

He turned to Emma with a grin. 'That makes sense, doesn't it?' he said.

Then, he pulled down the ear flaps of his leather helmet and shifted his goggles from the top of his head, down over his eyes. With a roar, they were off, waving and thanking Police Sergeant Goldfinch. Emma giggled as the side-car bumped up and down. She held on tightly as they turned corners. It was more like a ride at a fair, than anything else she had ever experienced.

The motor-bike's engine struggled a bit, as they climbed the hill towards Mount Fields.

'He'll be asking us to get out and push, soon,' said Mum, in Emma's ear.

'Expect, we're heavy,' said Emma.

Gradually, and with some last slow bursts from the engine, they were at the top of the hill and driving through the gateway to the old people's hospital. A jeep was at the front door with a group of nurses in their white aprons and caps, crowding round. Two young soldiers stood at a distance, looking concerned.

The motor-bike screeched to a halt and Mum and Emma climbed out of the side-car. Mr Cooper quickly took off his leather helmet and goggles. At that moment, a tall lady in a dark blue uniform, a little white apron and cap, and black stockings and shoes, came down the steps from the hospital.

'What nonsense is going on here?' she demanded to

131

know. The nurses backed away, obviously frightened of this strict-looking lady.

'Out you come, my dear,' she commanded, through the door of the jeep. 'No nonsense.'

Emma heard Aunt Bertha's voice replying, very firmly.

'You might as well know, Matron,' she said, 'that I am *not* coming into your hospital.'

'You have no choice, my dear,' said Matron, and opened the jeep door.

Mum looked very anxious, not sure what to do. Like the nurses, she was scared of Matron. Mr Cooper walked across to the jeep.

'Good evening, Matron,' he said, in his most charming voice.

She was obviously taken aback when she saw him there.

'This old lady is being *very* difficult,' she said.

He poked his head inside the jeep.

'Hello, Nanny Bertha,' he said. 'Nice to see you — but sorry to hear about the house. I've brought your niece to see you. Have a chat to her whilst Matron and I discuss a few things.'

He beckoned Mum and Emma to the jeep. 'Here they are,' he said to Aunt Bertha and then led Matron away in a very gentlemanly fashion.

Aunt Bertha's face was a picture of grim determination. There was no twinkle in her eye today, just a steely glint.

'Right,' she said to Mum. 'If I can come home with you, I'll get out.'

Mum looked very upset. 'I'm sorry, Aunt Bertha,' she said, 'that just isn't possible.'

'Don't you want me?' returned Aunt Bertha. 'Is that it?'

'No,' said Mum, even more upset. 'We just haven't room.'

'What's the matter with the front room?' she demanded to know.

'We've got to sleep there,' explained Mum desperately. 'There's no roof on the house and we can't use the bedrooms.'

'She'll give up fighting now,' thought Emma.

But no — 'Then these charming young men can drive me back to my own house,' she sounded as if the decision was final. 'I am *not*, my girl, definitely *not*, going to stay in Mount Fields with that dragon in charge.'

She leaned out of the jeep door. 'Come along, young men,' she called to the young soldiers. 'Take me home.'

The young soldiers did not know what to do, but they were saved by Mr Cooper. He and Matron returned to the jeep. *She* stood back, Emma noticed with surprise, whilst he went to speak to Aunt Bertha.

'Now, Nanny Bertha,' he said. 'I have a lovely idea. If you will get out, we can discuss it.'

Aunt Bertha gave him a suspicious look. Would she refuse to get out?

He said again, in a firm, quiet voice, 'Get out, Nanny and come with me.' He took her hands and, for the first time, her face looked unsure.

'Come along. Don't you want to hear my plan?' he enticed. 'If you don't know what it is, you'll never know the treat you're missing.'

She still looked suspicious, but her curiosity got the better of her and she allowed herself to be lifted down. Sighs of relief echoed round the group. Mr Cooper took her arm and gently led her to a seat, away from the crowd. He beckoned Mum to follow.

Matron spoke quickly to the nurses. 'Back inside and on

with your work,' she ordered. She followed them up the steps and whilst they hurried away, she hovered around just inside the door. Emma could see her, but Aunt Bertha could not.

The two young soldiers climbed back into the jeep. 'Bit of a character, your Grannie,' said one.

'She's certainly got guts and a sense of humour,' said the other. 'Need more people like her, now the war's on.'

'She's not my Grannie,' protested Emma. 'She's my Great-Aunt. Are you going?'

'Yes, they might need us somewhere else,' said the driver.

'Could you wait a minute, or two?' pleaded Emma, amazed at her daring.

'No need to,' said the driver.

'Please,' said Emma. 'If she sees you go, she'll think everyone's plotting behind her back and she won't agree to Mr Cooper's plan.'

'Doesn't have much choice, does she?' laughed the driver.

'Well no — not really,' replied Emma. 'But let her *think* she's making a decision.'

The other soldier laughed too. 'You cunning little minx,' he said. 'Trying to out-wit your old aunt, are you?'

'Not really,' protested Emma, 'but she's got to go *somewhere.'*

'I wouldn't want to live here with that old battle-axe,' said the driver. 'Worse than our sergeant-major.'

'If she agrees,' said Emma, 'It will only be for one night.'

'O.K. We'll wait.' They relented, but did not have to wait long before Mum, Mr Cooper and Aunt Bertha came slowly towards them.

'Give me my bag out of the jeep, please, young man,' said

Aunt Bertha. The decision had obviously been made and the soldiers handed the bag to Mr Cooper.

'Hope you'll be very happy, Mrs Wills,' said the driver, 'wherever you're going.' The jeep drove off.

Mr Cooper helped Aunt Bertha to climb the steps into the hospital. Mum and Emma followed. To their surprise, when the Matron met them at the door, she was charming.

'I am so glad that you have decided to spend one night with us,' she said to Aunt Bertha.

'One night and one night only,' was the firm reply. Aunt Bertha turned to Emma and Mum.

'You can go home now,' she said. 'I'll be quite happy and comfortable. Perhaps you could visit me on the farm sometime.'

Mum gave her a kiss, Emma followed and then thankfully walked towards the door.

'I don't understand,' said Emma, when they reached the bottom of the steps. 'I simply do *not* understand.'

Mum gave a chuckle. 'All of that sweetness is to impress Mr Cooper,' she said. 'He'll never have her in his home for a month, or two, if he thinks she's going to be difficult.'

'His own home?' Emma was surprised. 'Why is he doing that?' she asked.

'Well,' explained Mum. 'Aunt Bertha was his nanny when he was a young boy. That's how she met Uncle Frank — he worked on the farm and she, in the house.'

'I didn't know that,' said Emma, astounded.

'Long before your time,' laughed Mum. 'But Mr Cooper knows her pretty well, and is really quite fond of her. She was very important to him as a child, because his mother died when he was about four. She really brought him up.'

'Strange how things work out,' said Emma.

'I'm jolly glad he came along at that moment,' said Mum, 'otherwise I really do not know *what* would have happened.'

With huge feelings of relief, they quickly walked home.

Chapter Eighteen

BED IN THE SHELTER

As THEY walked down the alley by the side of the house, Mum and Emma heard the sounds of a trombone and cornet busking out:

> 'Kiss me Goodnight, Sergeant Major,
> Tuck me in my little wooden bed
> . . .'

Fran and Jonty were singing at the tops of their voices.

'If Bill thought that would send them to sleep,' laughed Mum, 'I think it's likely to do just the opposite.'

Emma giggled at the raucous sounds.

'Good job Dad's not here,' she said. 'He doesn't like them blasting forth.'

They opened the back door and the playing stopped abruptly. As they went into the living room, Bill said.

'Thought it might be Dad. The kids have enjoyed the performance, haven't you?' He dug Jonty in the ribs and Jonty responded — 'Great,' he said. 'You can go out again, Mum, and leave the boys to look after us.'

'Can I?' said Mum, with a smile. 'Come on, it's bed time.'

'Little do you know, young Jonty,' thought Emma, 'that

137

Jimmy won't be looking after you again — not ever.'

Mum was talking to her. 'You have your supper,' she said, 'if the boys have saved you some. I'll put Fran and Jonty to bed in the shelter, then we'll swap. You go into the shelter with them, and I'll have my supper.'

'Where are *we* sleeping?' asked Bill, as he and Jimmy took out their mouthpieces and put their instruments away.

'On the floor here, with Dad,' said Mum. 'We'll have to push the table back and get mattresses and blankets from upstairs.'

'Three mattresses,' said Bill, 'That'll be a bit of a squash.'

'I know, but you'll manage,' said Mum.

'It'll only be for two nights,' said Jimmy, 'and then I'm off.'

'Course you are,' Bill exclaimed. 'I'd forgotten that you'll be going so soon. Coo — I'll miss you, Jim.'

138

'So will we,' said Fran and Jonty.

'And me,' thought Emma.

'Come on, bed, you two,' said Mum and she whisked them off into the kitchen to wash and get undressed.

Emma followed to get her shepherd's pie out of the oven. She carried her steaming plate back into the living room and the boys sat down at the table to talk to her.

'What happened?' asked Bill. 'You were back *much* earlier than I expected. When Aunt Bertha makes up her mind, she's pretty hard to shift.'

Emma explained what had happened in Chanters Lane and their good luck in meeting Mr Cooper.

'*You* had a ride on a motor-bike and side-car,' Jimmy sounded impressed. 'Lucky thing.'

'I'd like Dad to get one,' said Bill.

'It was a big enough squash in the side-car for Mum and me — I don't know how the rest of you would fit in,' said Emma.

'O.K. — no motor-bike and side-car,' accepted Bill, reluctantly. 'We'll keep walking and biking.'

'One day,' said Jimmy thoughtfully, 'I'll save up and buy *just* a motor-bike. Then, when I'm a bit older, I'll be able to ride down from Yorkshire to see you all.'

'Good idea,' said Bill. 'I'll do the same and bring Emma up to see you.'

'There we are,' said Jimmy with a grin, 'We've sorted out our future transport.'

They were all laughing, but stopped abruptly, as they heard a hammering on the front door.

'Oh no!' exclaimed Emma, 'What else can have happened?'

'I'll go,' said Bill and went into the passage, along to the front door.

'Come in,' they heard him say cheerfully and Emma's

heart stopped thumping. It was Jimmy's Uncle Charlie, arriving with a pile of clothes.

Jimmy looked in amazement. 'More clothes!' he said. 'I thought I'd lost them all in the old school.'

'You had,' said Uncle Charlie. 'That's what was worrying me.'

'Where did you get those?' asked Bill.

'I went back to the centre, explained what had happened — and made a new selection,' said Uncle Charlie, pleased, and surprised at his success.

'I wouldn't have guessed there were so many good second-hand clothes around,' said Bill, as Uncle Charlie unloaded the clothes onto the table. Hiding beneath them all, in a green bag, was a cornet.

'Thought you could borrow this for Saturday,' said Uncle Charlie as he handed the cornet to Jimmy.

Jimmy looked surprised. 'Where did you get it?' he asked.

'It's mine,' said Uncle Charlie. 'Can't carry around a euphonium — too big — so I've got the use of a cornet 'til the end of the war. Got to keep my lip in somehow.'

'That's great,' said Bill. 'Dad will need his and I was wondering what we could do.'

'Is your Dad home yet?' asked Uncle Charlie.

'No — we're not sure when he'll manage to get here,' said Bill. 'He's helping at the old school.'

'Perhaps I could go round and give a hand, later,' said Uncle Charlie, 'when I've had a chat to Jimmy.'

'Is there anything? Do I need to do anything? Or know anything, before Saturday?' asked Jimmy, unsure of himself and showing signs on his face that he was dreading the day.

Emma put down her knife and fork and said to Bill, 'Come on. Let's go upstairs and sort out some blankets.'

'Be careful up there,' called Mum from the kitchen. They went out of the living room and climbed the stairs, leaving Jimmy and his Uncle to talk.

They peeped into the back bedroom. It was gloomy and the edge of the tarpaulin flapped against the broken window. The floor and beds were covered in broken glass, dust and debris from the damaged ceiling.

'Oh gosh,' said Bill. 'Where on earth are we going to find blankets that are clean enough?'

'Come on,' urged Emma. 'Take the corners of the bed spread, fold them over, tie big knots and trap all the mess inside.'

They carefully removed the bedspread, loaded with dust and rubble, to a corner of the room and took off the cleanish blankets underneath.

'Leave them there until we've got some off the other beds,' suggested Emma.

They collected six blankets and three pillows and went back downstairs. Emma opened the door into the living room and poked her head round. The room was empty.

'They've gone,' she said to Bill in surprise.

Mum came out of the kitchen. 'Yes, they've gone for a walk,' she said. 'Charlie had a few things he wanted to discuss with Jimmy.'

'Hope there aren't any more problems,' said Emma. 'As Saturday gets nearer — the harder it gets for Jimmy.'

'Where are Fran and Jonty?' asked Bill.

'In the shelter, nearly asleep,' replied Mum.

'I'll go in and stay with them, whilst you have your supper,' said Emma and went out of the back door. She climbed into the dingy shelter and sat on her bunk.

'Hello, Em,' said Fran, sleepily. Jonty was already fast asleep.

' 'Night Fran,' said Emma. 'I'll sit here, so you shut your eyes again.'

In the silence of the shelter, Emma watched the flickering candle flame. She was not sure, at this moment, whether she was lucky — or not.

She was lucky to be alive.

Lucky that no members of her family had been killed, or injured.

Lucky that the house had not been destroyed.

Lucky that she was *never* bored.

Lucky — she hesitated in her thinking — that she knew Jimmy better and was sure he liked her.

Was she really unlucky?

When she thought of the terrible things that had happened in the last few days, she could not convince herself that she had been unfairly treated at all.

She lay back on her bunk and was soon as soundly asleep as the little ones. She did not hear Jimmy and Uncle Charlie return, nor did she know of the discussions that took place round the living room table that night — until the morning.

Chapter Nineteen

MORE PROBLEMS FOR JIMMY

'ARE you awake?' Jonty's little voice piped up. 'I've been quiet for *ages.*'

Emma sat up, rubbing her eyes. 'Where's Mum?' she asked.

'Gone in to get Dad's breakfast,' said Jonty. 'She told me to stay here. Case I woke Bill and Jimmy.'

Fran sat up. 'Can we go in now?' she begged.

'Look,' said Emma, 'stay there. I'll creep in and ask if it's O.K.'

She pulled on her old coat, climbed out of the shelter and went into the kitchen. Mum was making toast for Dad and a boiled egg stood ready in an egg-cup. Dad was at the sink shaving, his chin covered in white foam, with his long shiny razor in his hand. He peered into the little mirror, which hung over the sink — and tried not to cut himself, as he drew the long blade down across his cheeks to his chin.

'Hello, love,' said Mum.

Dad turned. 'Nice to see you, Em,' he said. 'Missed you last night. So much keeps happening.'

'I've had a long sleep,' said Emma. 'Only just woken up. Can we come in? Are the boys awake?'

'I've just woken them,' said Mum. 'They'll have to get ready for school.'

'S'pose they're queuing for the sink,' said Emma, looking disappointed.

'Tell you what,' said Mum, 'Have some tea and biscuits in the shelter whilst you're waiting. You get back in and I'll hand it down.'

Reluctantly, Emma went back outside. It looked as if they were going to be stuck there until the boys had gone to school.

'If *only* we had a bathroom,' she thought. 'At least there

would be somewhere else besides the sink, where we could wash.'

She had another thought. The few people she knew with bathrooms, had them upstairs — so they'd be out of use anyway. Back in the shelter with Fran and Jonty, she left the door open, so that Mum could hand in the tea.

'Can we get up?' asked Jonty.

'Can we go in?' asked Fran.

'No — we've got to wait until Dad and the boys have gone,' replied Emma.

They both groaned.

'Why not?' asked Jonty, pouting.

'I'm fed up with being in here,' moaned Fran.

Mum appeared at the top of the steps with mugs of tea and biscuits.

'Don't be fed up,' she said. 'You've got a few more nights out there.'

They drank their tea, nibbled their biscuits — and waited. Jonty kept peeping out of the door.

'Here comes Dad,' he shouted.

Dad emerged from the back door and came across to the shelter.

'Morning, all of you,' he said. 'You certainly slept well out here. Not a sound all night — Mum said.'

'Can we come out, Dad?' pleaded Fran.

'In a few minutes,' said Dad. 'Mum will call you. The boys are almost ready.'

'They need to be,' said Emma. 'They've got to be at school by eight.'

The back door burst open and the two boys rushed out.

'Hello — Goodbye,' they called as they dashed through the gate.

'Out you come,' said Dad. They crawled out, kissed him

goodbye and went into the kitchen.

Mum had cooked four more boiled eggs.

'Scrummy,' said Jonty.

'Are they for us?' asked Fran.

'Yes, come on,' said Mum. 'I've shifted the mattresses and blankets out of the living room, so you can sit at the table and have your breakfast.'

She carried eggs, toast and tea into the other room. Fran and Jonty did not need telling twice to sit down and enjoy their breakfast treat.

'Emma,' went on Mum, 'You get washed and dressed first. They can get cleaned up *after* they've eaten their eggs.'

Glad to have the kitchen, and the sink, to herself, Emma quickly filled a bowl with cold water and added a dash of hot from the kettle. She washed, dressed and brushed her hair. Feeling quite respectable, she went into the living room to join the others. She lifted the egg cosy from her egg, and sat down to enjoy the nicest breakfast she had had for ages.

Mum bustled the two young ones into the kitchen to get them ready for school, whilst Emma sat with the wireless for company.

'Here is the news and this is Alvar Liddell reading it,' said the familiar, formal voice, that came from the large wireless in the corner.

'Last night, enemy planes attacked . . ., etc., etc.'

'We didn't get them,' thought Emma, 'but *somebody* did.'

Mum reappeared. 'Do you want to walk up to the school with us — and then I'd like to have a chat,' said Mum.

'Things keep changing . . .' and her voice trailed off.

'What's happened now?' asked Emma anxiously.

'Tell you later,' said Mum, 'when the little ones are at school.'

After they had seen Fran and Jonty into the playground, Emma got quite impatient to hear what had changed during the night.

The house?

The old school?

Aunt Bertha?

What could it be?

She stood hopping around, whilst Mum spoke first to the other mothers, then to Old Mike, who had brought the Shepherd children again.

At last they were walking back.

'What's happened?' Emma asked. 'Can you tell me now?'

'Well,' said Mum, 'it's Jimmy's Grandma — she's been taken into hospital.'

'Anything serious?' asked Emma.

'Charlie thinks it could be,' replied Mum. 'He had a telegram yesterday afternoon and phoned the church minister to find out more. She's got to have an operation and they are not sure how she'll be after that.'

'Must be serious,' said Emma.

'They think so,' said Mum. By this time they had reached the house.

'Let's make a cup of tea before we talk any more,' said Mum, as she opened the back door. She lit the gas under the kettle and washed two mugs under the cold water tap.

'That'll do for now,' she laughed.

'Mum's got more to tell me,' thought Emma. 'She *never* just washes things under the tap, she always waits for the kettle to boil. Wonder what it is?'

As they sat down at the living room table with mugs of

tea, Emma asked, 'What about Jimmy? Will he still go to Yorkshire?'

'That's the problem,' replied Mum anxiously. 'That's what I want to talk to you about.'

'Uncle Charlie took Jimmy off to explain it all to him and when they came back, we all sat and talked for ages. Fortunately, Dad was home by this time.'

'I suppose,' said Emma thoughtfully, 'she can't look after Jimmy if she's ill. Can he go to Uncle Charlie's family?'

'Well, for a week, or two,' replied Mum, 'but when his Gran comes out of hospital, the doctors have said she mustn't live alone, so *she'll* have to go to Charlie's family.'

'I see,' said Emma, suddenly realising what the problem was. 'There won't be room for Granny and Jimmy.'

She thought — 'Jimmy has nowhere to go!'

'Can't he stay with us?' she burst out.

'That's exactly what we were talking about last night,' said Mum. 'The problem is — our house. At the moment, we haven't even got space for us — let alone Jimmy.'

'It would be nice to have him here,' said Emma, feeling quite warm and happy inside. '*Can* we do anything?'

'Well, Dad's going to do some sorting out today,' said Mum. 'If we could get the roof repaired, within the next couple of weeks and the bedrooms cleaned up, we'd be O.K.'

'But what will happen in the next two weeks?' asked Emma.

'The idea is,' replied Mum, 'that Jimmy goes to Yorkshire tomorrow with Uncle Charlie, just as they'd planned.'

Emma's face dropped.

'Hold on,' said Mum. 'He will come back! Charlie has

148

fourteen days' leave — partly to sort out Jimmy's problems, and partly because his mother is seriously ill.'

'So,' Emma jumped to the rest of the story, 'for the next two weeks, whilst his Gran's in hospital, Jimmy will stay with Uncle Charlie's family — and we can sort the house out.'

'Exactly,' said Mum.

'Is Jimmy pleased?' asked Emma. 'Or is he disappointed?'

'He's pleased to be going to Yorkshire to see his relations and sad that his Gran is ill,' said Mum. 'But, I think he's happy to be coming back to live with us.'

Emma smiled. 'I'm glad,' she said, 'that he's not going for good.'

'He may go later, if his Grandma gets better,' Mum cautioned, 'so don't think he's going to be here for ever.'

'Promise — I won't expect that,' said Emma. 'One thing about the war — you can't rely on *anything*. All the time — things change.'

Mum agreed. 'One other thing, before we get on with the work,' she said. 'We must all have baths tonight.'

Emma looked shocked. 'How on earth are we going to manage that with Jimmy here?' In her excitement, she had forgotten about the practical problems of someone living in the house.

'Well,' said Mum. 'Dad, Bill and Jimmy will be at band practice tonight. You three can have your baths in the kitchen and go to bed in the shelter, before they come in.'

'What about you?' Emma asked.

'I'll do the same,' replied Mum. 'They'll be pretty speedy baths — in and out, one after the other.'

'Sounds O.K.' said Emma. 'I'm feeling pretty dirty.'

'You'll feel worse after we've cleaned out the larder,' laughed Mum. 'Remember, you have to go to school this afternoon.'

'Unless Tug-Boat Annie stops it!' said Emma.

Chapter Twenty

THE DREADED DAY GETS NEARER

WHEN Emma left the house to go to school, Mum made her promise that she would go the road way — *not* through the orchards.

'Promise, Mum,' said Emma. 'I'll probably meet the boys coming home.'

She hurried off expecting to meet them, but reached the school playground and still had not caught a glimpse of them.

'Odd,' she thought. She looked round and saw only girls. So she walked across to peer into the other playground. Maybe they had gone to talk to the airmen. They were not to be seen. Added to that, there was also a big notice up, under the arch —

OUT of BOUNDS
to all
BLANKTON BOYS AND GIRLS.
Signed: Mr Sparke — Miss Cannon

Emma was puzzled and stood wondering where on earth the boys could be, when, to her delight, she saw a little parade of cats coming towards her.

'Moggy's cats going for their dinner,' she thought. She

watched them go through, beyond the OUT of BOUNDS notice. The last cat rubbed against her legs and she looked down.

'Ginger,' she exclaimed and she bent down to pick him up. He purred and she said to him, 'We forgot all about you yesterday. *None* of us thought of you.'

She gently stroked his back. 'It's happened to you twice,' she whispered. 'Poor Ginger.'

The bell rang. She put him down and said, 'See you again.' He ran off to catch up with the other cats — she, to catch up with the girls who were already filing into the boys' school.

The afternoon drifted on. Emma knew she was not listening to lesson after lesson. Something was bothering her. In the middle of German she had a sudden inspiration.

'Ginger,' she burst out.

'I *beg* your pardon,' said Miss Swinton. 'How can Blau be ginger?'

The rest of the class laughed and Emma blushed. She stammered, 'I'm sorry, Miss Swinton. I wasn't listening. I made a mistake.'

'I *know* you weren't listening. I *know* you made a mistake. Ginger, indeed!' said Miss Swinton in disgust. 'Tell her, girls.'

'Blue,' they all said and turned in their desks to stare at her and grin.

Fortunately, the bell rang just then. Emma had never felt so thankful to hear it.

'Stehen,' said Miss Swinton. 'Auf wiedersehen.'

'Auf wiedersehen, Fraulein Swinton,' chorused the girls. She left the room.

Peggy turned round and said, 'Emma, what on *earth* were you thinking about?'

The others crowded round to hear her reply.

'The cat,' she said. 'Moggy's ginger cat.'

'Don't understand,' said Peggy.

'That's where Jimmy and Bill have gone,' Emma explained. 'Back to the old school to find Ginger.'

'They did go off in that direction when they came out of the playground,' said Peggy. 'Tommy went with them.'

'That's the second time they've tried to rescue him,' Emma told the girls, 'and got *me* into trouble.' The story about their first, successful rescue of Ginger, came tumbling out — finishing off with the letter of apology to Miss Cannon.

'But,' Emma said, 'they won't find him this time!'

'How do you know?' The girls wanted to hear more.

'Well, I've seen him,' said Emma, 'parading into *our* playground with the other cats, to be fed by the airmen.'

'How do you know it was *the* Ginger?' asked Virginia in her most scornful voice.

'Moggy's cats don't usually purr when you pick them up,' replied Emma, for once not put off by Virginia's lofty, scornful voice. 'They hiss and scratch. This one *purred* — and loved being stroked. I *know* it was Ginger.'

The other girls were smiling and nodding. They knew Emma was right. They *wanted* her to be right — and Virginia wrong. Her lofty tone was not popular with any of them, but they were a little bit afraid of this Miss Know-all.

'You'd better get home fast,' laughed Peggy, 'and tell the boys.'

Emma ran off, laughing inside at what had happened. That cat had caused some trouble!

'Where are the boys?' she asked, as she went in the back door.

'Having supper,' said Mum. 'Remember, it's band practice tonight. They were *very* late home from school. I

153

was quite worried about them.'

Emma went through into the living room. Jimmy and Bill looked up at her with sad faces.

'We've lost Ginger,' said Bill.

'Think he was killed in the old school,' added Jimmy, sadly.

Fran and Jonty looked as if they were going to cry.

'You haven't lost him,' burst out Emma. 'He's not dead.'

'How do you know?' They were all clamouring for more.

'He's gone to join his friends — Moggy's cats,' Emma told them triumphantly and went on to explain how she'd seen him — and what had happened in the German lesson.

Mum did not look pleased about *that*, but everyone was delighted to know that Ginger was safe.

'Can't wait 'til Monday,' said Jimmy. Then he stopped, as he remembered. 'I won't be here,' he added slowly and his face dropped.

'I'll give Ginger a stroke,' said Emma, 'and tell him you *will* be back.'

'Thanks, Em,' said Jimmy and cheered up.

'Come on boys,' said Mum. 'Get yourselves ready. Dad's not coming home, but going straight to the band room, so you'd better be off.'

Soon they were rushing around, washing hands, collecting instruments and disappearing out of the door.

'Good job Jimmy's not going to Yorkshire tomorrow, for ever,' thought Emma, as she sat at the table, eating her supper. 'I've hardly seen him today.'

Mum began collecting plates and taking them into the kitchen.

'We'll wash up and by that time the water in the copper*
will be hot enough for baths,' she said. 'Be ready, you two,'
she called to Fran and Jonty.

Emma went into the kitchen to help and soon everything
was washed and put away.

'Help me carry in the bath, Emma,' Mum said and they
went into the garden, lifted the big, zinc bath down from its
hook and struggled with it into the kitchen. Mum pushed
one end under the tap of the copper and began to fill the
bath with hot water. She then lifted bowls of cold water in
from the sink, until the temperature felt right.

'Come on, Jonty, you first,' Mum said. Fran and Emma
stayed in the living room, listening to Jonty splashing and
laughing in the bath.

'The water'll be a bit dirty when it gets to me,' said
Emma. 'And even _worse_ when Mum jumps in!'

'If we had a bathroom like Aunty Dot, we'd only have to
pull out a plug — then start again with clean water from the
tap,' said Fran, thoughtfully.

'But we haven't,' said Emma firmly, 'so we have to go on
emptying it out with jugs and bowls.'

'Will we _ever_ have a bathroom?' asked Fran, anxiously.

'I don't know,' said Emma, 'but remember, Fran, we
know more people _without_ a bathroom, than _with_ one.'

Jonty burst through the kitchen door, shining and clean,
and in his pyjamas with a big jersey on top.

'Come on Fran, you next,' called Mum and they could
hear her lifting bowls of water from the bath, and pouring
in more hot and cold.

Finally, they were all clean and drinking mugs of warm
cocoa, whilst Mum had her turn in the zinc bath. When she
emerged from the kitchen, she was dressed again quite
properly.

* Large metal container for heating water.

'Thought the others might bring someone in with them, so I'd better look respectable,' she said, as she sat down and enjoyed her cocoa, before she went back into the kitchen to empty more water.

'We'll leave it now until Dad and the boys come,' she said. 'Let's talk about tomorrow.'

They all sat round the table, hands under chins, to listen.

'Straight after breakfast,' said Mum, 'I want you three to go up Hollow Lane to Aunty Dot. She *is* expecting you. Fran and Jonty, you are going to stay up there all day, but Emma, you can come back and have dinner here.' She turned to Emma.

'I thought you'd like to come to the station with us to see Jimmy off,' she said.

'But the station's bombed,' protested Emma. She had just remembered.

'That's the East station,' replied Mum. 'They'll have to go from the West. It'll take a bit longer to London, but at least they'll get there.'

'And they've still got to get another train to Yorkshire,'

said Emma. 'They'll be jolly tired when they get there — but at least Jimmy will have plenty to keep him occupied.'

'He'll need that,' said Mum. 'It's going to be very hard for him.'

'What's happening to the rest of you in the morning?' asked Emma, choosing her words carefully. She *could* not use the word funeral — it was too painful.

'Uncle Charlie will fetch Jimmy, so that they can go together in the car,' replied Mum.

'Jimmy going in a car?' exclaimed Jonty.

'Yes, but rather a sad, black car,' said Mum. 'It'll be a miserable ride for him.'

'What will happen when you arrive?' asked Emma, anxious to know, even though she would not be at the service.

'It's been agreed that Jimmy can sit with the band in the church,' said Mum. 'It's a bit unusual, but everyone knows it will be easier for him that way. His Mum and Dad would have understood . . .' Her voice trailed off and her face looked very upset and miserable. Emma realised that it was going to be a hard day for Mum as well — Mr and Mrs Turner had been her friends.

'Where are Jimmy and Uncle Charlie having dinner?' asked Emma, desperately trying to talk about something different.

'Here, of course,' said Mum, her face looking a little happier. 'I thought you'd like to be with us.'

'Why can't we?' protested the two little ones.

'Sorry,' said Mum. 'Not this time. Dad will fetch you later.'

'Will he let us ride down Hollow Lane with him on his bike?' asked Jonty.

Mum looked horrified. 'You can't all get onto one bike,' she said.

'We can,' said Fran. 'Me on the back and Jonty on the cross-bar.'

'Glad I've never seen you,' said Mum. 'Now, you three — bed.'

'In the shelter *again*,' moaned Jonty.

'Yes,' said Mum firmly. 'In the shelter *again*.'

Chapter Twenty-One

NO FUN AND LAUGHTER

THE little ones were soon asleep, but Emma tossed and turned. She heard Dad and the boys arrive home from band practice. She heard the back door open — and close.

'There didn't seem to be anyone with them' she thought. 'P'raps I'll be able to go in for a little while.'

Then she remembered the bath in the kitchen. Shortly afterwards, she heard them carrying it outside and emptying the remaining water onto the garden. It was carried back in — and she knew that the second session of baths had begun. There was no way that she could go back in.

She tried to sleep, but could only think about the next day. She vaguely remembered the funerals of her grandparents, but they had seemed old. She was sad, but not shocked.

This time it was *young* people she was thinking about — her friend Betty, Mr and Mrs Turner, and the little ones. It could so easily have been *their* family. It could have been her, or Bill, in Jimmy's place. These terrible thoughts kept rushing through her mind. She was glad, when much, much later, the shelter door opened and Mum came in ready for bed.

'Mum,' she whispered.

'Did I wake you up?' asked Mum.

'No,' replied Emma. 'I haven't been to sleep yet.'

'You'll be tired tomorrow,' said Mum gently. 'It won't be an easy day.'

'I know,' said Emma, nearly crying. 'That's why I can't sleep — thinking about it.'

Mum gave her a hug. 'Listen,' she said, 'Jimmy needs us all to be calm tomorrow. Let's think only about him, so that he knows, all through the day, that we understand and are there to help *him*.'

'I'll try, Mum. I'll try,' said Emma, beginning to feel better now that Mum was here to talk to.

'I know you will,' said Mum and gave her another squeeze. 'Can you sleep now?'

'Yes, I can,' said Emma and snuggled down under the rough blankets.

It was a quiet night — no siren, no Tug-Boat Annie, or guns and droning planes to wake them up. Emma stirred, aware that Mum was getting up. The two little ones were still sleeping.

'Can I get up too?' Emma whispered.

'I'll bring your clothes out,' Mum whispered back. 'Get dressed here before you come in. There's not much room in the kitchen for cooking, washing *and* dressing.'

Mum brought the clothes. Emma dressed quickly and joined her in the kitchen.

Three mugs of tea stood steaming. Dad was, once again, covered in frothy shaving cream, his long, shiny razor in his hand.

'Hello, love,' he said. 'I hardly saw you yesterday. You'll have to wait for a kiss!' he laughed.

'Don't think I want mouthfuls of that,' Emma said with a

grin. She felt better this morning and more able to cope with the day ahead.

'What about the roof?' she asked.

'Some of my mates are going to start on it after work this morning,' replied Dad. 'I'll help them tomorrow — and see how we get on.'

'You and me, Emma,' said Mum, 'are going to spend tomorrow cleaning up the bedrooms. Bill can look after Fran and Jonty.'

They sipped their tea as they talked. Mum stirred the porridge and cut bread for toast.

'Watch this,' she said. 'Make sure it doesn't burn, whilst I go and wake up the little ones.'

As Dad finished his shaving, Bill poked his head round the door.

'Any tea?' he asked.

'In the pot,' said Dad. 'Come and help yourself.'

Bill filled two mugs and carried them back into the living room. Emma could hear him and Jimmy talking. She felt shut out, somehow, and wished *she* was a boy. But there was no time for brooding. As she heard the table being pushed into place, she knew that the blankets and mattresses had been carried upstairs.

Mum appeared with the little ones from the shelter.

'All change,' called Dad. 'Boys in the kitchen to wash and dress, everyone else in the living room for breakfast.'

They shunted around. Bill and Jimmy, with clean clothes in their arms went into the kitchen, whilst Mum and Emma carried toast and bowls of steaming porridge into the living room. It seemed ages before the boys were ready to join them at the table.

'It could only have been about ten minutes,' thought Emma, telling herself off for being so silly — caring that time was running away.

Saturday, the dreaded Saturday, had arrived. She would not be sharing the morning with the boys and she was glad. Then dinner — the station — the train— and she would be waving goodbye to Jimmy. He *would* be coming back, Emma reminded herself. She could not help feeling secretly glad that his Grandma was ill. Then she felt guilty and really did hope that she would get better — but not yet!

The boys finally emerged from the kitchen looking smart and clean.

'Right, boys,' said Dad. 'Breakfast.'

'I think just toast for me,' said Jimmy, as he sat down. Emma looked at him, but he was just looking down at the table, not wanting to meet anyone's eyes.

Mum said, 'That's O.K. Jimmy. Carry on with the toast. I can make some more, if you need it.'

'I — I won't need it,' said Jimmy, hesitantly. 'I'm not really hungry.'

'Don't worry, boy,' said Dad. 'Just eat what you want.'

'Fran and Jonty, go and wash your hands, because you're going with Emma in just a few minutes,' said Mum.

'So soon?' questioned Emma. To her own surprise, she knew she was glad to be going — quickly. She *could* not sit here and feel the pain that was Jimmy's. 'How is Bill going to manage?' she thought. Her admiration of Bill, grew.

Without a word, Emma followed the little ones into the kitchen to wash her hands. There was a knock at the front door and she heard Uncle Charlie's voice.

'It's all starting,' she thought. 'I must go.' She was almost ashamed of her feelings of desperation as she rushed to get herself and the little ones ready.

'Say goodbye,' said Mum, looking at her anxiously. 'You don't need to say *anything* else,' she whispered.

Emma stood in the living room doorway.

'Bye all of you,' she said awkwardly. Dad blew her a kiss from where he stood with Uncle Charlie.

Jimmy raised his eyes and said, 'Bye Em. See you later.' He looked down again and went on slowly, very slowly, munching a piece of toast.

Fran and Jonty were not quite sure why everyone was so subdued and unhappy this morning. There was no fun and laughter — even Bill had not teased. In fact, he had hardly spoken.

Emma took them along the alleys to Hollow Lane and told herself that she *must* make it a happy day for them, however she felt inside.

'Race you to the dips,' she said and they all ran to the little path that wove its way above the high walls of chalk that enclosed the road. They trampled on grass, wild flowers and tree roots, as they followed the path, until they came to the first dip.

They carefully climbed down the chalky face to the bottom. Huge lumps and little pieces of chalk were all around, amongst the bushes, flowers and grass.

'Mind the stinging nettles,' Emma said.

'Can we take some chalk with us?' asked Fran. 'Aunty Dot's got a big blackboard we can draw on.'

'O.K.' said Emma. 'Two pieces each. Not too big. You've got to carry them!'

She picked up two more pieces for herself and they scrambled back up the chalk to the little path at the top. As they emerged at the other end and wound their way back down to Hollow Lane, they heard an awful wail. The siren sounded faintly in the distance.

'Oh no! Not now,' said Emma. 'Come on, you two. Run quickly to Aunty Dot's.'

They rushed along, glad when they at last reached the

top of the hill. Aunty Dot was waiting for them on the doorstep.

'I'm glad you're here,' she said. 'I got worried when I heard the siren.'

She looked at their white shoes and hands.

'I know where you've been,' she laughed.

Emma turned and looked back over the fields towards the city. The barrage balloons were rising into the air and floating around below the clouds like whales. The cathedral peeped up in the distance, isolated now, not surrounded by roofs and chimneys.

She heard a faint bellow. 'Tug-Boat Annie,' she exclaimed. 'Why *did* they have to come this morning?'

'Into the shelter,' said Aunty Dot.

'Can I stop and look, just for a minute?' pleaded Emma.

'O.K. I'll take Fran and Jonty down,' said Aunty Dot, 'if you *promise* to come when things start happening. It might all seem a long way off, but bits do fall around up here.'

She whisked the two little ones away and Emma looked up as she heard the drone of planes. In a V shape, they came. Above and below, smaller planes were diving up and down. Guns sounded — small guns at first — then big, thumping sounds.

'Those are the sort of guns that go up and down the railway line, on trucks,' thought Emma.

The heavy planes avoided the city centre, protected by barrage balloons and Emma could see them flying away into the distance.

'I wonder where they're going,' she thought. 'But I'm so glad they've left us alone today.'

Tug-Boat Annie sounded its deep note of 'All Clear' and Aunty Dot came out of the shelter, followed by Fran and Jonty.

'The siren won't give the "All Clear" until later,' she said, 'when the planes have dropped their bombs and disappeared over the coast.'

'Hope they don't come back this way,' said Emma.

'Come on,' said Aunty Dot. 'These two want to use their chalk and you can help me in the kitchen.'

Time passed happily. The siren sounded its 'All Clear' and Emma began to relax, as every hour passed. This dreadful Saturday morning would soon be over for Jimmy.

She was delighted to hear Aunty Dot saying, 'Nearly time for you to go. Let's have a drink.'

They had glasses of orange and ginger biscuits, then they came to the door to wave goodbye to Emma, as she set off back down the lane.

Chapter Twenty-Two

EMMA'S SECRET

EMMA turned a bend in the road and saw Jimmy coming towards her.

'Hi,' he said.

'Hello,' she said with surprise. 'Where are you going?'

'To meet you,' he said with a grin. 'I needed to go for a walk — and thought I might as well come this way. Do you mind?'

'Oh no,' said Emma. 'I'm glad.' Inside she thought, 'I'm very, *very* glad.'

They started back down the hill together.

'I'm very relieved this morning's over,' said Jimmy slowly. 'I loved Mum, Dad and the others very much — and I *hated* saying goodbye to them that way.'

'I would have felt the same,' said Emma.

'Thought so,' said Jimmy. 'That's why I wanted to see you.'

They walked on in silence for a few minutes — each unsure of how to break it — what to say next.

'Race you to the dip,' Jimmy said and they both rushed off, scrambled up the chalky bank and stood laughing amidst the chalk, weeds and bushes.

'This feels so *normal*,' said Jimmy. 'I like it.'

He bent down to rub some of the white dust off his shoes.

'Forgotten I've got to look respectable to go on the train to Yorkshire,' he said, pulling a face.

'Use my hanky,' said Emma. 'Doesn't matter if I'm a bit messy.'

As he gave his shoes a rub, they were both startled by a magpie. It swooped out of a tree towards them, dropped something shiny into the bed of stinging nettles and flew off.

'What on earth's that?' exclaimed Jimmy. He crept cautiously towards the stinging nettles.

'Get me a stick, Em,' he said. She found a short, thick branch and handed it to him. He started to beat the nettles until they were flattened. Then he peered down.

'Come and look,' he said excitedly. She joined him and there, peeping out from between the nettle roots, was something silver and shiny.

Jimmy wrapped Emma's handkerchief round his hand

and carefully, very carefully, stretched towards the object. As he lifted it out, they saw it was a watch with a silver bracelet strap. He looked at it in amazement.

'But — that's just like my Mum's,' he said. 'It can't be hers. Can it?' He turned the watch over and read on the back —

'To Elizabeth. Lots of love, Fred.'

'That *is* hers.' He could hardly speak. He was stunned by this find.

Emma stood beside him quietly. 'Why here?' she thought. 'How could the magpie have known?' She had heard about miracles, but had never expected to experience one.

Jimmy was talking again. 'Dad gave it to Mum when they got engaged, so it's rather a special watch.'

He was turning it over in his hands as he spoke.

'What a miracle that the magpie dropped it here — now, at this minute,' he said.

'That's just what I was thinking,' said Emma. 'It must have seen it shining in the rubble and carried it off in its beak.'

'I hadn't thought about the *things* in our house,' said Jimmy. 'They didn't seem to matter, somehow. But this is different.' He paused — and then said, 'Pity, I'm a boy.'

'Why?' asked Emma. 'You like being a boy.'

'Usually,' he said, 'but I can't wear the watch.'

'You can put it away in a safe place,' said Emma.

'That's not what watches are for,' replied Jimmy. 'Mum did that — and look what happened. Nothing's safe any more.'

He looked at the watch quietly for a few more minutes.

'Tell you what,' he said, looking serious. 'Will *you* look after it for me?'

'Me?' Emma was startled — but thrilled at the thought.

'You were here when it was found. You knew my Mum. Betty was your best friend — and she would have had it one day,' he said. He paused another minute.

'*I'd* like you to have it. It's been marvellous for me, having you to share things with this week,' he said. 'Whatever happens in the future — I'll never forget.'

He handed her the watch. 'Please, Em,' he said.

She took it. 'Thanks, Jimmy,' she said, 'for wanting me to look after it for you. But, will you promise me one thing? When you want it back to give to someone else, please ask.'

'I promise,' he said. 'Now — a promise from you. If you get so busy with other boys as you get older, that you really don't care about me, and my Mum's watch, will you give it back?'

'I promise,' she said solemnly.

The watch was now on her wrist and he took her hand. 'That's a bargain, young Em,' he said. 'We'd better get moving, otherwise there'll be no dinner before we go to the station.'

They moved off the chalk dip back to the road.

'Don't let's say anything about the magpie story, when we get back,' said Jimmy. 'Let it be our secret for now.'

'Can I tell Mum and Dad later?' asked Emma.

'Yes, when I've gone,' he said. 'I think Uncle Charlie *would* understand, but I don't know him quite well enough yet.'

Emma pulled the sleeve of her blouse down and hid the watch. 'No-one will see it now,' she said.

He looked. 'No they won't,' he said, 'but *we'll* know it's there.'

They reached the house and went in.

'Come on, you two,' said Dad. 'We were just about to start eating.'

He looked down at their shoes.

'I know why you've been such a long time,' he laughed. 'You can't resist those chalk dips, can you?'

Soon they were all eating and everyone seemed more relaxed, as if the time apart had been good for them. Uncle Charlie and Bill had been playing duets and Dad had been helping Mum in the kitchen.

'I won't come with you to the station, if you don't mind, Jimmy,' Mum said. 'Whilst you were out, Dad went across to the phone box and spoke to Mr Cooper — just to find out how Aunt Bertha is.'

'My wife doesn't like using the phone,' Dad explained to Uncle Charlie.

'Neither does mine,' said Uncle Charlie. 'Says she doesn't know what to say, but normally, she never stops talking!'

He grinned at Dad. 'It's these new-fangled things,' he said.

'Well, how is Aunt Bertha?' asked Emma. The men were teasing Mum. Things were getting back to normal.

'She's fine. Settled down well,' replied Dad, 'but she'd like to see Mum, to talk about a few things in her house.'

'Mr Cooper has said he'll come and fetch me,' said Mum.

'Another ride in the side-car,' said Bill, enviously.

'Your turn will come,' said Dad.

'We've decided,' said Jimmy, 'Bill and I are going to buy motor-bikes one day, so that we can get around the country.'

'Well, it's trains we need to think about now,' said Charlie, looking at his watch.

Emma had to stop herself doing the same.

'Silly,' she thought. 'It's not even going! Hasn't been wound up for a week.' Going or not, the watch felt good hiding under her sleeve.

The bustling started and before many minutes had passed, they were walking down the street towards the station. Dad and Uncle Charlie went ahead, carrying the cases and Bill, Jimmy and Emma behind.

'It'll be odd going back to Yorkshire,' said Jimmy. 'I remember the day we came down — just Mum and us children. Dad had already been down a few weeks to sort out a job and a house.'

'Why did you come?' asked Bill.

'Well, Dad was out of work, and discovered that they needed miners down here. That's why.'

He went on, 'Mum didn't want to leave. I remember her crying as we left, although she tried to hide it from us kids.'

'But she *was* happy here, wasn't she?' asked Emma, anxiously.

'Yes, she was,' replied Jimmy. 'We all were. Now, the funny thing is, I feel as if I belong to Kent — not Yorkshire. I'm glad I'm coming back.'

'Come on, you three,' called Dad. 'We've got a long way to go.'

They had reached the bottom of York Road, when Billy's bus came bumping along Winfield towards them.

'Tell you what,' said Charlie, 'does that brown bus go near the station?'

'Well — yes,' said Dad and put his hand in his pocket to feel for money. 'We do have time to walk — just.'

Uncle Charlie put out his arm and the lumbering, old brown bus squeaked to a halt.

'On you get,' he said and offered Billy a shilling.

'Two and three halves to the station, please.'

'No trains from the East,' said Billy. 'Which do you want, South, or West?'

'West,' said Dad.

'Go on, find a seat,' said Uncle Charlie.

They made their way to the long, back seat.

'What a treat,' said Bill. 'We only go on a bus when we go to see Aunty Bess on Boxing Day.'

'The rest of the time we *walk* everywhere,' said Emma.

They bumped along in the back of the bus, passed rubble and ruined buildings, passed the lofty cathedral and Westgate that had remained undamaged, until they reached the bottom of Station Road. Clambering out of Billy's bus, they walked along to the station. Dad and Uncle Charlie went to get tickets.

Bill stood on the huge weighing scales. He had no money to put in, but it was fun standing there, looking up at the big face and hands that could tell him how much he weighed. He bounced up and down — but the hands did not move.

'Without money,' thought Emma, 'his weight remains a secret.'

She had begun to feel sad, now that the time had come to say goodbye. As she remembered her own secret, she felt happier.

Dad and Uncle Charlie came back and they all walked across to the ticket collector. Uncle Charlie shook hands with Dad and Bill and gave Emma a kiss — much to her surprise.

Jimmy shook hands with Dad and Bill — and gave Emma's hand a warm squeeze.

'Bye. See you all soon,' he said.

'Thanks a lot, all of you,' said Uncle Charlie, as they went through the ticket barrier.

The train steamed in. Bill, Dad and Emma watched as Uncle Charlie and Jimmy climbed on. They turned to wave goodbye.

'Come on through,' said the ticket collector. 'That's young Jimmy Turner, isn't it?'

'Yes,' said Dad. 'He's going off to stay with relations in Yorkshire for a bit.'

'Poor kid,' said the ticket collector.

'He's been very brave,' said Dad. 'Funeral this morning.'

'I know. My brother-in-law's in the band,' said the collector.

'Of course he is,' said Dad.

As they talked, the guard blew his whistle and waved his green flag.

Jimmy and Uncle Charlie leaned out of the window waving.

'Bye,' said Emma, waving back. As she did, she saw something silver and shiny peeping out from beneath her sleeve and suddenly, felt happier.

"That's a lie," I told ... what ... as they went
on, ... the ... begin.

The train came to a ... the ... trains ... two as
I ... home and he ... car out of ... the ... that's a ...
journey.

"... enough," said the elder woman. "That's
the first thing I've ...

"No," said the ... in a ... of ... who ... to
me ... at the ...

"Yes," ... said the older ... "Yes.

"If you ... not ..." said ... to ... the ...
"I hope ... he ... is there in the ... for ... and the
...

"I ... we ... and I ...

As they talked ... I could not ... and ... and ... the
... in ...

"I wish," ... I ... to ... the ... and ... to be ... his
journey.

Sleep and figures were ... as he ... I was ...
... myself ... and they ... the ... to be ... a ...
... somewhere ... people left ... and ... as a ... to ...